BANDIDO REVENGE

"I am Shelter Morgan, late of the Confederate States Army. If any among you will join us, we will seek these bandits and kill them all."

"Brave words," the girl on the steps jeered. "If you mean them. But among these . . . these rabbits, you will not find one with *cojones* enough to accept your offer, *Señor Gringo*."

"Don't be so quick to judge, miss," Shelter began, with Raul translating. "Give these men time to find themselves. If I am not mistaken, a powerful gun that fired rapidly many times without reloading was used in the attack, right?"

"How do you know this?" Maria Elena asked suspiciously.

"We are seeking the bandit leader known as El Guillo. In particular, I am after the American who owns and uses that gun. It is my intention to kill him. If El Guillo and his bandits get in the way, then they will also be killed."

A sudden smile lighted the girl's face and Shelter realized how much more beautiful she was than he had previously considered. "You speak well. There is much to tell. Come, rest in our town, stay the night. Tomorrow you can ride on. Hopefully some of the men of El Crucero will find their lost courage and accompany you. I am called Maria Elena."

"*Con mucha gusta, Señorita,*" Shell managed on his own.

#18

SHELTER

TABOO TERRITORY
By PAUL LEDD

ZEBRA BOOKS
KENSINGTON PUBLISHING CORP.

ZEBRA BOOKS

are published by

KENSINGTON PUBLISHING CORP.
475 Park Avenue South
New York, N.Y. 10016

First printing: May, 1984

Printed in the United States of America

1.

Songbirds filled the air with inviting music and a woodpecker made a rapid-fire assault on the bark of a tall Douglas fir that stood well back from the banks of the Sacramento River. Although the placer mining had long-since played out, the surrounding hills had become dotted with the low, black openings of mines, some active, others abandoned when they showed no color. So skillfully did the tall, lean, dark-haired man move through the forest that his passage did not disturb the winged and furry inhabitants. In one fist he held a long-barreled .44. His quiet stalk attested to his infinite patience. Yet, there was a quality of smoldering restlessness about him, a driving will that had been forged in a hotter fire than any a blacksmith had ever encountered. He was the very personification of a man with a mission.

The weapon in his hand left no doubt that the task ahead would be fraught with violence. Only the question of time and place remained. In a matter of fleeting minutes, he had the answer to that.

"C'mon, ya old fart," a growling voice came to him from among the trees. "We know ya stashed that poke somewhere. You're gonna tell us where, no matter."

The hunter heard the sound of a blow and a quickly choked-off grunt of pain. Another meaty fist smack hushed the birds and squirrels.

"Nate, bring me one o' them limbs from the fire. We toast his balls a little and he'll open up, I'll bet."

"No! Please. Not that," an older voice, strained by misery

5

and fear called out.

Hatless now, the stalker had moved into a position where he could see the clearing. One gray-haired man lay sprawled near the center in the twisted-limb posture of death. Another had been tied to a tree on the opposite side. Blood trickled from a split lip and dark welts of bruised flesh had begun to discolor on his cheeks. Two others occupied the open space at the front of a small mine tunnel. One was a complete stranger. The other, Nate Lewis, was known only too well to the unseen bringer of violence. At sight of the weak, narrow face with its effeminate pouting lips, wide-set eyes and receding chin, brought a boil of anger to the watcher's chest. Quickly, while Nate brought a smoking length of wood from the fire, a plan formed.

"Please. Oh, please don't do that," the grizzled miner wailed.

"What are you whinin' about, old man?" the torturer sneered. "Those cods of yers ain't worked in ten years, I reckon. Ain't like yer losin' yer best friend."

"You done killed *him*," the aged miner moaned. "Now just do the same fer me and let it end."

"Not till we know where that gold is."

Hot embers singed tender skin and a yowl of agony came from the bloody lips of the helpless man. "I'll tell, I'll tell. Take it away."

"That's more like it," Nate Lewis snarled. "Make it fast."

"It's buried. Real deep like, under the fire ring. Figgered nobody'd ever look for it there."

"You better be tellin' it straight, old man, or we'll burn your pecker off so it looks like you got two belly buttons."

Gleefully the two robbers went off to scatter the fire and dig at the ground below. As they labored, the stalker swiftly worked his way around the clearing to the tree where the old-timer had been bound. A quick flick of a Bowie blade and the ropes fell free. He helped the miner to his feet and eased him out of the way, to a place of safety. Then he stepped into the open and started to walk toward the thieves.

"Dig, damnit, dig," Lewis' partner yelled, driven to a frenzy by the thought of hidden gold.

"I am. Why don't you help?"

"There's only room for one, idjit."

Suddenly the spade in Nate's hand struck something resistant that gave off a scraping, metallic sound. "That's it!" he shouted in excitement.

They dropped to hands and knees and clawed frantically at the dirt, unmindful of the hot ground. Nate pried a corner of a tin biscuit box loose and they scrabbled with more energy.

"Here it comes! Here it comes!" Nate's partner in crime yelled. Then a shadow fell across the ground in front of them. The petty outlaw dropped his end of the treasure box and clawed at the grip of an eight-shot Rupertus cartridge pepper-box tucked in a wide, soiled red cloth sash around his paunchy middle. He pulled the awkward weapon free and started to bring it up.

A two hundred five grain bullet spit from the muzzle of the Colt .44 and removed two rodent-like buck teeth from the thief's mouth before it shattered the first cervical vertebra and unhinged the killer's skull from his spine.

"Oh, Jesus! It's Cap'n Morgan," Nate Lewis gulped as he dived for his Dimmick-Colt percussion revolver.

Shelter Morgan pumped a .44 slug into Lewis' shoulder, which sent the aged six-gun flying. Lewis flopped onto his back and tightly clutched the wound with his left hand, while blood seeped between his fingers. He began to whimper.

Morgan stepped forward without a word, toed Nate's hand away from the entrance wound and ground the heel of his boot into it.

"Ow! Oh, God, don't hurt me, Cap'n. Please. I . . . I thought you was dead."

"So did a lot of people. Most of them are now. You know why I'm here?" It was more a statement than a question.

Lewis gulped and swallowed with difficulty, then nodded slightly. "T-the gold, ain't it? The gold we took from you in Georgia."

"The gold you murdered and committed treason against the Confederacy for."

"Hey, Cap'n. Hey, you gotta believe me, sir. I di'n see a penny worth outta that. Them officers cut it up between 'em. We got short shrift on that one, an' that's the truth."

In Shelter Morgan's mind, the images of unavenged ghosts whirled and cackled at this. They knew, as did former Confederate Army captain, Shelter Morgan, that Lewis lied. More than forty men shared in the quarter million in gold that he and his patrol had risked their lives to bring safely out of Tennessee under the very noses of the Yankees. Naturally, the portions of the officers had been larger, but even a worthless private who couldn't shoot straight and had two left feet like Nate Lewis got something out of their betrayal. Brooding anger suffused Morgan's face with dark crimson.

"*Please*, sir. Don't kill me. I didn't get anything. W-why else would I be robbin' poor miners if I had a big stash of gold?"

"You're lying." Again the heel bore down into the seeping wound. Lewis screamed. "You make a shithouse smell like roses, Lewis. No doubt you spent it all, like a lot of others too stupid or too lazy to make it work for themselves. I'm going to kill you, Lewis, like I have so many of your fellow vermin."

"Oh, God!" Lewis blubbered. "Oh, please, please don't kill me. I . . . I wanna live. I didn't do nothin' wrong. Please!" Lewis gasped and gagged, hands clasped prayerfully in front of him, despite the pain in his shoulder. "I . . . I can help you. Tell you where some others are." A shifty, calculating glint came in his tear-watered eyes.

"Which others? I've evened the score with so many you might be giving me the address of a corpse. Talk, damnit!" Morgan stomped the bullet hole again.

Lewis turned sheet-white and nearly lost consciousness. Only a thin wail of agony escaped from his girlish, colorless lips. When he regained control, he gushed out his news in a rush of words designed to save him from eternal darkness and torment.

"Tom Plaskoe. You remember him, don't ya, Cap'n? Sergeant Tom Plaskoe, t'one from Captain Packard's company?"

Morgan's eyes hardened. He recalled a slackard NCO who usually wore a soiled, frayed uniform, even before the privations of war had put them all in rags. A sergeant who held his position by dint of his fists and brutal punishments and exerted the least effort necessary to escape criticism or demotion.

"Yes. I remember Tom Plaskoe."

"Well, ya see, he's out here in California, too. Down by a place called San Diego. He has a gold mine up in the mountains near the town of Julian."

"A gold mine?" Yeah, Shelter thought. What better way to pass stolen gold?

"So help me. I ran into him once, I was down on my luck. When I recognized him, I hit him up for a little. He offered me a job at this mine, the Dorado he called it," Lewis produced a sly smile. "But robbin' 'em is easier, so I said no. He staked me to fifty dollars, said the times had been good to him."

"He's still down there?"

"Far's I know."

"Instinct tells me I should kill you outright. Lord knows you deserve it for the good men who died that day. What you've told me is worth something, though."

Lewis' hopes flared, then died rapidly as Shell went on talking.

"I'm gonna turn you over to the old man here. He can take you down to Sacramento and have the authorities hang you. You'll get to live a few days longer that way. Just to know you're going to swing will be satisfaction enough for me." Shelter turned and started to walk over to the badly beaten old man.

Suddenly the grizzled miner raised an old Maynard percussion rifle to his shoulder. To Shell it appeared as though he might be the target. He leaped to one side as the antique bellowed and belched out a big sixty-nine caliber ball.

Behind the vengeful ex-Confederate, the conical lead projectile made a meaty smack and Shell heard a brief cry of pain, cut off in the middle as though by a headsman's axe. He spun around and saw Nate Lewis sprawled on the ground, a large portion of his skull missing on one side, with blood and brains pouring from the opening. Near the tips of his right hand fingers lay a Remington No. 4 derringer. Lewis' legs twitched spasmodically for a long moment, then his body heaved convulsively and he lay still.

"Never turn your back on a rattlesnake ner a polecat," the old miner advised.

"Thanks, mister. I know better. Just miscalculated with this one."

"Do that often an' ya won't be able to make mistakes again."

"A point well taken. Are you going to be all right?"

"Yep. Could use some help buryin' that trash an' my partner, though."

"Obliged to you. I'll be more'n willing to give a hand. By the way, have you ever heard of this Dorado Mine?"

"Nope. But I can tell you where Julian is."

"That will help. Let's get the chores out of the way, I'll fix us something to eat and you can fill me in."

2.

Pedro Ruiz saw them first. At ten years of age, Pedro had been herding goats for two years for the *Patron*, Don Alexandro Portales. Pedro took great pride in the trust placed in him and the importance of his occupation. Barefoot, the hard soles of his feet callused until only the sharpest of cactus thorns could penetrate, he slowly strolled out of town along the narrow dirt road that connected El Alamo with distant Tecate, on the border with *Los Estados Unidos del Norte*. The goats grazed over a lengthening space each day, so that Pedro knew that by the time he reached his eleventh birthday, he would be making at least a five mile jaunt to find them new grass and shrubs to consume. Think of it! Five miles out on one side of the road and five back on the other, all so that the goats would be sleek and fat and provide delicious *cabrito* for feast days and *fiestas*. Pedro's contemplation of his notable contribution to the community was interrupted by the appearance of two men.

Dark complected and grave of visage, they sat in their high saddles and looked down on him. They wore twill trousers and *cortero* jackets like wealthy dons and the huge sombreros of *caballeros*. Twin cartridge belts criss-crossed on their chests. Pedro snatched the straw sombrero from his head and clutched it with both hands in front of his thin breast.

"*Buenos dias, Señores.*"

"*Muy buenos, niño,*" the larger one replied in a deep voice. "Is that the village of El Alamo?"

"Yes, it is. And I am called Pedro Ruiz, the goatherd."

"*Con mucho gusto*, Pedro Ruiz. I am called El Guillo."

11

Pedro's sun-darkened face blanched pale as the flesh of his belly. El Guillo was a name he knew and one to be feared. He swallowed with difficulty and bobbed his head.

"I am honored, *Señor.*

A short, barking laugh came from El Guillo. "You know me, then?"

"Everyone has heard of El Guillo," Pedro told him truthfully.

"Indeed . . . Indeed? Well, then, Pedro Ruiz, go about your work. *Adios.*"

"*Adios, Señor El Guillo.*"

El Guillo and his silent companion turned their horses about and cantered off. Instead of following the big man's instructions, Pedro left the goats to fend for themselves and ran, fast as his short legs would carry him, to the village.

"El Guillo! El Guillo is coming," he shouted as he neared the first small, low adobe houses. "*Ayudame Dios! Los bandidos!*"

The small boy's cry galvanized the town. Men ran from their work to seek what weapons they possessed. Rifled percussion muskets appeared from mantelpieces, shotguns in plenty and even two aged flintlock rifles of dubious make and quality. Under the direction of the *alcalde* and the lone village policeman, carretas, ore wagons and buckboards were rolled into place at the ends of the two streets in town. Three strong young men hurried to the charcoalers and returned with heavy bags of oak charcoal, which they used to fill the wagon boxes. Others tried to stack adobe bricks to make some sort of barricade. Pedro ran on to the church to inform Padre Luis.

"Stay here, boy," the priest advised him. "I must gather the women and other children and bring them in for protection."

"I can help, Padre. I guard the goats all day. I am strong and fast."

Padre Luis patted Pedro on the head and gave him a warm smile. "That you are, *niño.* Be swift, then. We surely have little time." The priest dipped fingers in the holy water fount, as did Pedro, crossed himself and left the small church on his mission

12

of rescue and preservation.

From a hilltop overlooking El Alamo, a richly and colorfully dressed band of forty men watched the town's pitifully inadequate preparations to resist their onslaught. Under the wide brims of their *charro* sombreros, beady black eyes glittered with greed. El Alamo had a copper mine and, rumor had it, gold had recently been discovered in a gorge near the village. All the better for them when the looting began. A light breeze ruffled the luxurious mustaches that drooped around their thick-lipped mouths and flickering smiles of amusement at the ant-like antics of the villagers livened their otherwise grim features. Their leader, Rudolpho Santacruz, the one known as El Guillo, pointed a finger at the church.

"Observe, *compañieros*, that the women and children are being put into the church. We are not Yaqui *indios* who are frightened by superstitious dread. The church we will leave for last. That way we can take our time enjoying the tender flesh of those lovely birds, no?"

Slightly larger than his companions, El Guillo enjoyed a special status as a bandit leader. Silver conchos lined the outer seams of his trouser legs and thick silver braid weighted down his large sombrero. He wore a brace of old Colt Dragoon pistols, a machette and six thin-bladed, double-edged daggers that he could throw with equal skill to his use of them in his hand. At forty-three, he had started to put on a bit of a pot belly, though his five foot nine stature still hid it somewhat. At the squeaking sound of ungreased axle hubs, he smiled, revealing tombstone slabs of yellowed, crooked teeth.

"The *gringo* has at last arrived," he announced to his men.

Most of the Mexican outlaws had little liking for the American, but he had something that made him precious beyond all personal feelings. He had what he called his "toy."

A stout carreta labored up to the crest and the driver halted a drooping headed mule who propelled it.

13

"Hi, Rudy," the American called to El Guillo. "Where do you want me to put it?"

El Guillo winced at this discourteous use and overly familiar shortening of his Christian name. He grunted and shared his black scowl with his *amigos*. Then he pointed down the rutted little road to a place some two hundred yards from the town.

"Right there should do it, *Señor* Plaskoe. My men and I will divide and come in from the east and west sides of town."

"How about blocking off escape to the south?"

"Come now, *Señor* Plaskoe. Although my men are brave as *el tigre de la montañas*, who among even them would be foolish enough to stand in front of that *monstroso* of yours?"

Tom Plaskoe produced a whimsical smile. "Yes, there is that. Well, I had better get on with it. And, uh, Rudy, call me Tom, eh? After all, we are partners."

"That is not necessary, *Señor* Plaskoe. You are a guest in my country. Courtesy demands a certain, ah how do you say? A certain formality."

El Guillo's cold rebuke was lost on Tom Plaskoe. He reseated himself on the carreta.

"Manuel, Ricardo, let's go," Plaskoe called to the youngest two bandits, whom he had trained as a crew for his toy. Although he could work it alone, its efficiency was increased by using the proper number to operate the big gun.

The Mexican outlaws, hardly more than boys, kneed their horses into place ahead of the carreta without making comment. Plaskoe lifted the reins and slapped them against the mule's rump. With the painful shriek characteristic of its class, the two-wheeled vehicle rattled off down the road.

Plaskoe's pale, nearly colorless blue eyes glittered with anticipation. He enjoyed these violent excursions, relished the terror his toy created. Most of all, he appreciated the power it represented over even these deadly men who rode with El Guillo. They might hate him, but his command of such an awesome weapon kept them in line. When he drew up to the place indicated by the bandit leader, Plaskoe studied the hastily erected barricade.

He would have to do this in two setups. First deal with the barrier, then move in closer to work on the town. Manuel unhitched the mule while Ricardo busied himself setting out the long-handled swab and other implements. He filled a leather bucket with water from a barrel lashed to the side of the carreta. Then Plaskoe crawled into the back of the vehicle and removed a tarpaulin from the stout pedestal and multi-barreled tube of a 1.1" bore Gatling gun.

Manuel handed him a box of cartridges. Plaskoe set them aside and turned the big crank, dry-firing the weapon through all six barrels. Then he tore the paper box open and fed the five-and-a-half inch long shells into the hopper on the top of the Gatling. He added a second box while Ricardo took his position as trainer. It would be his responsibility to aim the Gatling gun while Plaskoe fired it.

"To the right a little," he told Ricardo. "To the right. *Al derecho*," he repeated in Spanish. "Good."

Plaskoe's hand rested lightly on the crank, then he began to turn it. A heavy roar, as of thunder, filled the air. As the powerful slugs spewed from the six rotating barrels, a gigantic cloud of powder smoke obscured first the road, then the entire town.

The huge, blunt-nosed bullets smashed into tables and carts. Wood splinters maimed the defenders of El Alamo and a huge ball of dust rose from instantly pulverized charcoal. One man caught a slug in the chest. It struck with such power he hadn't even time to scream before he flew to one side and flopped lifelessly on the ground.

After fifteen rounds, the frightful weapon fell silent. Plaskoe added another box of ammunition to the hopper while Manuel swabbed the barrels. One more burst, Plaskoe thought, and I'll run some cornmeal loads through to give the barrels a good cleaning.

"Clear," Manuel told him.

Again the crank rotated and death screamed into El Alamo.

The brave townsmen fell like windrows of wheat, mercilessly cut down while everything disintegrated around them. Their nerve had nearly broken when the Gatling gun ceased firing. Cautiously, three of the survivors poked heads above the barricades. They started to take aim when, with a chorus of wild screams, the bandits of El Guillo charged into the village from two sides.

"Harness the mule!" Plaskoe yelled.

While Manuel hurried to the task, Plaskoe emptied the hopper into the backs of the men, now turned to meet this new threat. Bodies and chunks of torn-off meat flew through the air and screams of the dying rose in dreadful refrain. When the last round cleared the chamber, Manuel and Ricardo rapidly hitched the mule and the Gatling gun advanced to the riddled barricade.

A bullet whined off a metal fitting on a wagon stake near Plaskoe's face. Instinctively he ducked, then rushed to the Gatling. "Up there," he shouted to Ricardo, pointing to the belfry of the church. "There's two or three of 'em."

The young bandit trained the gun and Plaskoe splashed the adobe tower with big 1.1" slugs. The violence of the impacts set up a sympathetic resonance in the bell. Chips of adobe clouded the air and the big brass bell gave off its last, mournfully off-key note when a huge lead ball smashed into it. A moment later, a villager pitched forward out of the arched opening and tumbled to the hard-packed soil of the churchyard.

Another, his right arm ripped off by the big bore Gatling, fell screaming to his death on the tile floor inside the church. Plaskoe ordered the aim changed and began to sweep the fronts of buildings down the main street. He paused every fifteen rounds to have the barrels swabbed to prevent powder fouling and ran six cornmeal loads through after each thirty for a more thorough effort. Though they chambered with some difficulty, the delay insured the frightful gun would continue to rain destruction on the hapless residents of El Alamo. Plaskoe hummed with delight as pieces flew from the fronts of buildings, or the tall, narrow, carved doors disintegrated under the powerful assault of the big Gatling.

Plaskoe had to take greater care now that El Guillo's men rode through the streets smothering all resistance. A fire had started, he noticed, in one house at the far end of town. Only a few rifles spoke in defiance of the marauders. Wails of terror came from the windows of the church. One bandit charged into the main street, chasing down a running man. He reined up sharply at sight of the Gatling gun and threw a snap shot at the fleeing townsman.

The bullet clipped the villager at the waist. He screamed in agony as his legs ceased to function and he hurtled into an adobe wall. With his death, silence came to El Alamo.

A dozen laughing, chattering bandidos rode up to the steps of the church.

"*Hola*," El Guillo called to the priest. "Open the doors and let the ladies come out where we can enjoy them, priest. Do it now or we will break them down and it will go badly for you, I can guarantee."

"This is the house of God," the Padre's voice came strongly from inside. "Go about your evil elsewhere and leave us in peace."

"Sorry, Padre, but we can't quite do that. The church is rich, it has much gold. Surely the Pappa in Rome will not miss what little you may have inside there. It is ours now. We wait to come and claim it."

"Sacrilege! Go now before your souls are eternally damned."

"I am sorry for you, Padre. You leave us no choice. *Oye, gringo*. Bring up your marvelous gun."

Mutters of prayer and the wailing of children and frightened women came from the church while Plaskoe's crew harnessed the mule again and the Gatling made slow, squeaky progress down to the small plaza and lined up outside the church. Plaskoe dumped a box of ammunition into the hopper and turned the crank.

At first the thick oaken slabs of the double doors resisted. Then splinters began to fly and a large portion of the middle crumbled into a shredded hole.

"Stop! For the love of God, stop!" the priest cried out. "You're killing innocent women and children."

El Guillo made a sign. "It is all right now, Padre. We can get in to take what we want. *Andale, muchachos*."

Quickly the bandits herded the women and children out into the plaza. Then they went about stripping the altar, statues and reliqueries of all valuables. While they did, El Guillo amused himself with a frightened, doe-eyed young mother of two.

"Bend over and grab your ankles," he demanded, the urgency of his excitement bulging the front of his trousers.

When the sobbing woman complied, he hoisted her skirts and jerked down the pantaloons she wore under them. With practiced ease, he undid his fly one-handed and hauled out his throbbing organ. With a grunt of effort, he thrust himself into her tightly constricted, dry passage. She screamed with pain.

"Aaah! This is what life is all about, *niñas*," he told the terrified, bawling little daughters of his victim. "All of your life you will find a man lusting after your pleasant warm bodies. Why, even now . . ." he paused to execute several deep jabs with his engorged phallus that brought new sobs and cries of agony from the wretched young mother. "Even now there are men among my *amigos* here who would hunger for your flesh, young and tender though it may be. As women," he went on philosophically, "it is your duty to satisfy men. As girls in the town of El Alamo, it will be your privilege to service El Guillo and his friends. Do you not tremble with happiness at such an honor?"

Tom Plaskoe sat atop his carreta and surveyed the women in the square. Five of them now lay on their backs, sobbing but offering no other resistance, as the unoccupied members of the bandit gang rutted on their bodies. At last he saw her and he felt his desire rise stiffly in his trousers. Yes. The exact one. A

18

beauty and not a day over fifteen. His lean, weathered face flushed with passion and he removed his hat. Nervously he ran long, slender fingers through his nearly white blond hair. The knife slash scar on his left eyelid itched and its droop accentuated. His heart raced in his chest as he left the seat and started toward the girl, who tried to hide herself behind a large woman with gigantic girth and pendulous breasts. When Plaskoe came close, she sensed his purpose and tried to dart away.

Lightning quick, Plaskoe's hand darted out and grasped her slender wrist. She shrieked and twisted in his grip as he pulled her toward his precious carreta. When he reached his goal, he hoisted her with ease and sat her small round bottom on the rough boards of the conveyance. He swiftly tied one trim ankle with thongs laced through a ring in one sidewall of the cart. He jerked the other one to the opposite side and secured it.

With a strong tug he ripped her skirt down the front and peeled it away from her body. Instantly, his eyes widened with appreciation.

"No underfrillies, huh? You must be a hot one." His lust had become a rigid pole swelling the front of his trousers and he massaged it with the heel of one palm to ease its discomforting demands. A stir among the captured women attracted his attention for a minute.

At El Guillo's direction, three of his men led the priest from his church and stood him against the small fountain in the center of the square. A ragged line of six other bandits formed in front of the Padre, who stood with bowed head, lips moving in silent prayer.

"Carga!" El Guillo's lieutenant, Pablo Sanchez, bellowed.

The men in the rough formation fed cartridges into their rifles.

"Apunto!"

Six bandidos took aim.

"I told you, Padre, what would happen if you refused to be reasonable," El Guillo interrupted the commands to call from where he continued to have his way with the sobbing young mother.

"Fuego!"

The six rifles cracked as one. The priest's body jerked and swayed with the impact, but he stood rigidly still for a long moment, blood streaming down his back and chest. Then, with a small sigh, his knees crumpled and he fell in a spreading pool of his crimson life fluid. Keening wails went up from the women and children. Tom Plaskoe rubbed his hands together in a gesture of finality and satisfaction and turned back to the girl.

"Another task taken care of. And now for you, my lovely little thing."

He opened his trousers and exposed a small, though rigid, penis that better fitted the body of a boy of twelve than a man of thirty-five. He crawled into the wagon and positioned himself between the crying girl's legs. At the last moment he gave thought to the situation and hastily bound her hands behind her back. Then he lowered his reddened shaft and forced it into her unwilling cleft.

She screamed, she wriggled and she bucked. Humming a tuneless melody, Plaskoe rode her like an untamed bronco, finding joy in all her exertions. Rapidly he pumped his hips and ground his way into her dry passage only to meet resistance which he quickly smashed through, using the seeping blood of her shattered maidenhood to lubricate his way. Now more pleasing sensations tingled in his body and began to have an effect on her.

Despite herself, the young girl started to experience shock-waves not of pain, but of pleasure. Her body grew sensitive to the slightest motion of the small, iron-stiff rod that plunged inside her. Waves of delight cramped her belly and sent trembles down arms and legs. Fear and loathing began to be replaced by an emotion she had never before experienced and her welcoming juices began to flow like never in her short life. She opened her eyes and saw the looming menace of the

Gatling gun directly above the bobbing head of the white-haired man who grunted and strained atop her. Idly she wondered if he ever let it out of his sight. Then she licked her lips and spoke softly to him.

"If you untied my hands, *Senor*, it would be much better for us both."

3.

Running late, as usual, the Southern Pacific train from Los Angeles to San Diego hissed and clattered its way along the track through rolling hilly land that was part of Rancho Las Penasquitas. It would reach its destination in another quarter hour. One passenger, though his calm, handsome face did not reveal it, itched with impatience.

Shelter Morgan longed to recover his horse from the livestock car up front and be on his way to Julian. Nate Lewis had told him that former sergeant Tom Plaskoe had a mine there. From what he had learned of Julian, it would be a two day trip from the harborside town of San Diego to the small mountain village. Once more, images of a tall, lanky young tow-head sergeant with oddly colorless eyes filled his mind.

Tom Plaskoe spreading a silently crying drummer boy of thirteen over a wagon wheel for punishment for some petty infraction. Company street whispers reached then-Captain Morgan that the facts had it the boy was being grated for refusing to ease Plaskoe's tensions from being too long without a woman. Morgan put no weight to it at the time.

Another flash of Tom Plaskoe, wearing civilian clothes and sitting near to Major Twyner, smoke belching from the muzzle of his Starr revolver while the slug tore off the ear of a good man, Private Bill Keane. Poor Keane had gone insane later on and, though Shell had been unfortunate enough to be the one to rectify that situation, he basically blamed it on that fateful day in Georgia when General Custis, Colonel Fainer and the others decided to traitorously trade in their Confederate gray

22

for glittering gold.

Yes, Shell Morgan wanted very much to hasten the next meeting between himself and Tom Plaskoe.

"San Diego," the conductor called as he walked through Shell's car. "Last stop, S-a-n Di-e-go!"

Inevitably, Shell encountered a delay before the slat-door of the stock car rolled back and his big black trotted down the loading chute. He let the sturdy horse nuzzle his shoulder a moment, then slipped it a bit of fresh turnip and slung his saddle on the broad back. He loosely fastened the cinch and led the Arab crossbreed out of the railyard. Walking felt good, so Morgan proceeded up the main street to a small, tidy-looking hotel, where he took a room for the night. Next in order of importance was to wash the taste of coal dust out of his throat.

Shell picked a small saloon a short distance from his hotel and entered. Sawdust covered the floor, along with the hulls of goober peas, walnuts and almonds. A large, "free lunch" spread covered a quarter of the bar. Several tables were occupied by blue-suited sailors and some merchant seamen in red-and-white striped shirts held down three more. A flaring conical fireplace made of adobe blocks and lined with brick was built into one wall and jutted out into the room. Half a dozen local men occupied space at the bar. There were, he noted, a good baker's dozen of women of dubious virtue, but obvious occupation, decorating the establishment.

One of them, a raven-haired beauty with faintly olive complexion and the noble nose of Moctezuma, watched him closely as he strode across the crunching floor to the bar. She detached herself from the restraining arm and groping hand of a sailor and sauntered with a seductive wiggle of her hips toward where Shell stood. Her professional smile slipped and she replaced it with one of genuine welcome.

"Schooner of beer and a shot of real Kentucky bourbon, if you've got it," Shell told the apron.

While the bartender hastened to fill the order, the soiled dove reached her destination. "My it's nice to see a new face in

23

this place for once," she began in a low, throaty voice that reminded Shell of the gentle creaking of bedsprings.

"Would you buy a girl a drink?"

"I don't see why not, ma'am."

She peered into Morgan's deep blue eyes. "You're Southern, aren't you?"

"Yes, ma'am."

"I love Southern men. They're so . . . so *durable*."

Shell smiled and nodded his head slightly. "That term could cover a multitude of sins, ma'am." He raised his hand to place an order for her.

"I meant it to. And please, my name is Luisa."

"I'm Shell Morgan, Luisa. I must say you have a way of making a feller glad he chose this saloon."

"Ummm. I like that, Shell. Southern men are so . . ."

"*'Durable?'*" Shell teased.

"I was going to say gallant, but I like it better in my language," she amended, then added in Spanish, "*valiente.*"

"The way you said that word, Luisa, it was pure music."

Luisa tossed back her head and released a trill of light laughter. Her dark eyes flashed. "Spanish is a musical language. Listen; *vamanos a mi camma, corazon.*"

"I see. What does that mean?"

"Let's go to my bed, dear heart."

Shell blinked. "Now?"

"Would later be any better?"

Shell grinned at her and lifted his shot of bourbon toward his lips. A hammy hand closed on his forearm and interrupted the motion.

"The lady's spoken for, so get the hell away from her," the owner of the hand growled.

"Not by you," Luisa replied testily.

The broad shouldered man in the blue uniform ignored her remark and spoke again to Shell. "Shove off, Mac. This little chili pepper is mine."

"The lady said, 'no,'" Shell quietly informed him.

24

"You lookin' for the deep six?" the sailor snarled. "Sissy like you could get ground up into dog meat in a sailor bar."

Shell smiled nicely. "A loudmouth like you could get your ass kicked up between your shoulder blades almost anywhere."

Then he swung a short, chopping right across his body and smacked the sailor in the lips.

"Git him, Jake!" another sailor at the nearest table shouted.

Jake rocked back a step and tried a round house punch on Shell. Morgan flipped his glass of whiskey into the sailor's eyes. He had already taken his measure of Jake. He presented no major problem. In fact, he looked like he had been left up in the rigging for too long. He had big hands, wrists and forearms, but nothing much behind them. Particularly in the brains department, he seemed a few bricks shy of a load. By the time Shell had squared off facing him, Jake had wiped clear his eyes and decided to charge.

A bad mistake, as he quickly found out.

Shell set his feet and brought a sizzling left jab up from his toes. His hard knuckles found that spot behind the point of Jake's chin and before the sound of the blow had faded, Jake's eyes rolled up and he did a graceless pratfall on the sawdust-covered floor. He remained upright a second before toppling sideways, his cheek resting on a pile of peanut shells.

One sailor had proved easy enough to handle. The six who came boiling up from two tables, friends of Jake's, provided more action than Shell wanted.

The first made a wild swing and Shell grabbed his arm, using the sailor's momentum to whirl him around, then he threw the luckless combatant into the next two who tried to close on the bar. Shell had to change his position or be at a huge disadvantage, he knew, so he shifted left, cracked a short right to a sailor's cheek and shuffled away again. Two came at him at once and he grabbed up one of the chairs they had abandoned and hurled it at their chests.

One of them went down, hugging a sore jaw and split lip

25

where an oak leg caught him. The other brushed the chair aside and charged. The time for being a nice guy had ended, Morgan estimated. He waited until the last possible instant, then kicked the furious seaman in the crotch.

He went down with a whoosh of air and thin, keening cry of agony. His face turned red and he rocked back and forth, getting in the way of another swab who wanted a piece of Shell Morgan. The burly sailor managed to get around the gasping man on the floor in time to catch two solid punches to the chest and a quick jab that cut the skin over one eye. Shell danced back out of the way.

With a bellow of rage, a heavy-set sailor ran at Shell, doubled over, arms out wide to grab and squeeze in a bear hug. Shell side-stepped him and gave him a powerful kick in the ass that sent him windmilling across the floor and, with a shout of horror, head-first through a big sectioned-glass window. Two of his buddies launched themselves through the air at Shell.

Unexplainably to them, the table they tried to hurtle traveled along with them, the toe of Morgan's boot hooked around one leg. When their leap ran out of momentum, they fell face first into a welter of glasses and beer buckets. Before they could recover and get their feet on the floor, Shell rolled them off with solid fists to the sides of their heads. One of them came up with a knife.

"Shell, look out, he's got a knife!" Luisa shouted. In her excitement she repeated it in Spanish. *"Quidado, el tene un cuchillo!"*

That's the end of playing it fair, Shell thought as he reached under his coat and whipped the .44 Colt from his holster. It made a shattering blast in the confines of the saloon and brought silence.

The slug drilled a hole in the sailor's left shoe, a fraction of an inch from his second toe. He halted, eyes wide, and dropped the knife.

"You had better take care of your playmates here," he told the remaining sailor. "I don't like it when kiddies play with dangerous weapons. Sometimes I've been known to put neat round holes in them for it. Besides, I was developing a powerful urge to explore the nether regions of the lovely Luisa here when your friend Jake rudely interrupted me. Drag him out with the others and let me return to my examination."

"You fellers are goin' to pay for all this," the barkeep demanded.

"What do you mean?" the swab whined. "He's the one who busted most of it up."

"An' you and yer buddies lost the fight. In my book that means *you* pay. Or do I summon the policeman on this beat?"

The sailor looked sheepish. "Naw. Un-uh. No need for that. We'll settle up come payday."

"See you do, or your tabs are all canceled and I'll go to the Commodore about your not payin' yer bills."

"You have a nice room here," Morgan told Luisa some ten minutes later.

"Thank you. We are required to, ah, entertain gentlemen off the premises of the saloon. At least this way I am not in a four by eight foot crib, no? Now, it is my turn to thank you."

"What for?"

"That Jake Tilton is a *cabron*. A, how do you put it in English? A pig and a dirty slob. I would have had to go with him or lose my job if you didn't come along."

"The lesser of two evils?" Morgan teased her.

Luisa's eyes opened widely. "*Dios, no!* You . . . you are like a ray of sunshine on a rainy day. And this . . ." she went on as she began to unbutton her dress, "this is on the house."

The heat in Morgan's loins turned into a volcano. Its stiff central core rose to press urgently against his trousers and a slight tremble of anticipation surged through his lean body. His cinder cone of passion threatened to erupt and he hurried to ease the pressure by freeing that insistent shaft of flesh.

Pale gold, Luisa's skin came slowly into view as she shrugged

27

out of the gaudy costume of her profession. Creamy mounds of lush, full breasts billowed like gigantic rollers of a delightful ocean, a sea well capable of quenching even his raging volcano. Her smooth shoulders narrowed down to a tiny waist, then flared into inviting hips that promised much and revealed even more.

Only a sparse thatch covered her swollen mound, Shell noted with pleasure, and already droplets of moisture glistened in the cleft. She moved all together, sinuously, heightening his ardor as he speedily divested himself of the restrictions of clothing. Shell hung his gunbelt on the headboard of the bed and turned to face this delightful creature.

"What was it Jake called you? His chili pepper?"

Her quick frown soon melted as she examined his ready, vibrating flesh. "I am fiery, that you will soon see. Perhaps it fits. Though not from his mouth." Shell opened his arms and she came to him.

A lightning bolt of shared delight crackled between them as warm skin caressed coolness. They kissed and her flesh became the waves of San Diego bay, buffeted by a turbulent wind. Shell explored her crests and valleys with his tongue and fingers. Her touch at the nape of his neck, sharp fingernails trailing along his spine, soft, warm pads on the small of his back, strong digits grasping his flat, firm buttocks made his being soar like a schooner caught in a squall. Then she located his main mast and, with small, sure strokes, began to hoist sail. Still standing, though tossed as on the quarterdeck in a gale, she slathered the mighty pole in the juicy fronds of her outer chamber, then steeped that mast in a warm, clinging socket more secure than that of any mighty sailing ship of old.

"Mummmm," she cooed as she began to undulate her hips and insert more of his goodness. "Mummmm. You are my man forever. See? I put my mark on you."

Swiftly she leaned forward, rising on tiptoe, and bit him on the chest.

"Ow!" Shell cried. "That drew blood."

Like a good sailing master, he quickly adapted to the rhythm of the surging deck that plunged against his body and matched it stroke for stroke. The sloshing of the bilges made sweet music for his ears and the heady scent of her own enjoyment rose to tingle his nostrils.

Head swimming from these marvels, he heard the pitch of the wind increase to hurricane strength, howling in the room like all the lost souls. The howling, he realized, came from Luisa, who churned against him with such violence and hunger, ingesting every last inch of his powerful mast, that their pubic bones clashed in pleasurable pain.

At last, a timeless time after the amorous conflict began, she arched her back and shrieked like a northern gale while her body shuddered in fulfillment. On they labored, though, until Shell felt the tidal bore surge up in him and rifle down the long extension of his soul that plumbed her sweetest depths. The lunar surge exploded in a rich spray of foam that, for a brief while, doused all their fires.

"Next time, *corazon*, we might be able to wait until we get to the bed."

"Let's do that now, to play it safe," Shell suggested.

They lay side by side and already Shell Morgan felt stirrings in his groin and a languorous lengthening of his reddened shaft. Luisa saw it swelling and sent a hand to encircle that large love lance, skillfully squeezing and stroking it to fullness.

"You are in a hurry."

"No. It's you who make me rise to the occasion sooner than I expected." The dark rings around her rose-bud nipples fascinated Shell. He bent to kiss them and felt the nubs harden at his touch. One he worked with thumb and finger while the other he laved strenuously with his lips. His other hand sought that secret chamber that nestled between her thighs and he inserted two fingers to bring joy once more. Luisa didn't leave all the effort to her man.

Slowly she drew his rigid projectile into range and aimed it by unseeing instinct for its flight into the fantasy of her pulsating mound. Eagerly he aided her with a sudden forward thrust.

Slippery flesh enfolded him and he continued his dive into the grotto of her desire. Luisa threw a leg over his hip and made room for more of that throbbing mast to slide into its natural sheath.

"I think I wasted money on a hotel room," Shell panted out.

"How is that, *amo mio*?"

"I suspect I'm going to be here all night."

4.

It took all of the warm, humid night and part of the next morning to calm the storms in Shell's swollen weathervane. For her own part, Luisa exerted exceptional effort to heighten every experience for them both. Never had she enjoyed a man so thoroughly. Even her deflowering, at the age of twelve, aided by a *gringo* boy whom she dearly loved, had not been so exciting.

On the day after their first delightful, if somewhat dry and chaffing, experience, he had come to her all worried, his little *verga* all red and puffy, sore to the touch. He was afraid, he told her, that what they had done was bad and it would make his dingus fall off. Not so, she told him, they only needed practice to toughen it up. Then she eagerly cooled his fevered member with her lips and tongue. For one long, hot summer, the two children had made love two or three times every day, gaining in knowledge and skill. Then the boy's family had moved to a ranch near Campo and Luisa never saw him again. But her hunger had been awakened and the fires burned brightly. She soon found another boy, then another.

Not all of the throbbing organs she had encountered over the next seven years could extinguish that blaze. Then, like the shining knight of romantic Spanish poems, Shelter Morgan came into her life. She lay beside him now, wondrously sated, her slippery purse tingling and slightly sore from their multitude of encounters. Her eyes hungrily devoured his long, lean, scarred body and paused longingly at his groin.

Luisa's heart skipped a beat when she observed his indominable member, chaffed dark red by their marvelous friction, had already reached a state of semi-rigid arousal. Her hand sought it while she changed position on the sweat-damp sheets of her bed. Heart palpitating with excitement, she lowered her head until her long black tresses tickled his rigid belly. She enclosed the bulging tip in her mouth and, with all the skill she had learned that summer long ago, she used lips and tongue to draw it to fullness.

"Aaah," Shell sighed. "Yes. That's it. Take it deeper."

Slowly Luisa worked down the rigid staff, enscribing spirals all the while on that sensitive knob that pushed its way toward her throat. *Por Dios*, she wondered. Could she take all of it into her this way?

Her tongue cupped the bottom of his shaft now and, with little nibbles of her lips, she inserted more of his massive manhood. A vein on the upper ridge pulsed against the roof of her mouth and sent shivers of delight down her spine. She closed her eyes and began to hum a little Mexican tune.

The vibrations of her throat drove Shell wild. He writhed on the bed and thrust upward until her flexing lips encountered the thick tufts of hair at the base of his outsized maleness. Constant waves of blinding pleasure washed over him as she worked on. He could smell her own arousal and longed to plunge his lance deep inside that perfumed garden until they both fled their senses in pure enchantment.

At last, Luisa relented. "Now," she gasped when that mighty phallus had been removed from her mouth. "Take me now . . . hurry!"

Shell gladly obliged.

An hour later they sped to the heights together and cascaded over the precipice into sweet oblivion. When reason returned, Shell realized he must end this enraptured interlude. He rose from the bed and reached for his clothes.

"Oh, no, don't go so soon," Luisa pleaded. "You're the only man who has ever filled me to overflowing. I have never known such happiness."

"I came here to accomplish something important," Shell explained to her gently. "I can't get it done in this bed, no matter how delightful it is."

"What is this important something?"

"I have to find a man. Have you heard the name Tom Plaskoe?" He went on to describe him.

A frown of concentration creased Luisa's brow. A long moment of silence passed and then she pursed her lips. "Yes. I think so. White hair . . . even down there." She reached out and tweaked the long curve of his partly flacid penis. "A tiny *verga*, like a small boy. No bigger than this." She illustrated with her fingers separated about four and a half to five inches.

"He uses what little he has roughly, though. None of the girls like him to visit them. He is supposed to own a gold mine up near Julian. He pays well. That is all I know."

It verified what little Shell had from Lewis and told him an intimate bit more that he really didn't need. Then he recalled the rumors about the real cause of the drummer boy's punishment. Perhaps Plaskoe liked little girls and boys indiscriminately? It could be. Shell thanked Luisa while he dressed. She profusely heaped praise and thanks on him. At the door, he paused a moment and delved into his pocket.

"You're going to be expected to come up with the barkeep's share," he told her. "Take this, it should be enough." He dropped two double-eagles onto a small table.

"Oh, no, it is too much. I can take no money. It is I who should be paying you. You have thrilled me and made me feel so calm and happy inside like no one ever before. Come back to me, my precious Shell."

"I'll try," Shell offered.

"Better still, let us enjoy each other once more before you go."

Heat radiated from Shell's loins and his large organ sprang to instant attention. "Now that's the best offer I've had all

33

morning." Quickly he began to undo buttons.

Two more villages tasted the fury of El Guillo before the bandit horde headed northwest toward the border. A pair of buckboards had been filled with gold and other loot. They slowed their progress, as did the carreta with Tom Plaskoe's Gatling gun. The outlaws made camp early on the second evening, with only another day's journey to reach a safe crossing spot where prying American eyes would not see Plaskoe slip into the country with the loot.

While his men erected his tent, laid out the cooking gear and gathered wood for a fire, El Guillo remained seated on his horse. One hand idly brushed the small, hard cones of a young girl's breasts, while the other fished up under her skirt, the fingers probing her dripping slit.

"Well, my little *chiquita*, soon you will have my big, hot *chile* in this slippery place. What do you think of that?"

"I hope you are bigger than the *Señor gringo*. I could hardly feel him."

"Believe me, my cock could make ten of his. You will think you are choking to death when I ram it to you down below. *Ay!* You make me burn with the need. I can wait no longer. *Vamanos a chingada en los palos*."

"Yes," she simpered. "Let's go fuck in the trees."

Que bueno! And to think she is not yet fifteen. Eagerly, El Guillo led his willing prisoner to a small stand of piñon.

Tom Plaskoe sat cross-legged in front of a large pot of hot, soapy water. Meticulously he soaked, scrubbed and wiped dry the parts of his beloved Gatling gun. He had swabbed the barrels until they shined and the cotton cloth patches showed not the least trace of black. Now he worked on the finicky parts of the revolving mechanism. As he toiled, he lost all consciousness of the camp.

Lupe Aranza had an idea. Ricardo and Manuel knew how to make the big gun work. For what did they need the *gringo*, then? Whoever kills him can lay claim to that marvelous weapon. Why not him? Then he would ask Ricardo and Manuel to show him exactly what the *gringo* did to make the gun shoot, the young bandit considered. There he sat in his carreta, lost to the world, washing the parts of the gun like a woman did a baby's bottom. Such foolishness, Lupe scoffed. Silently, he drew a long, thin-bladed knife and approached Plaskoe's back.

Before the bandido could get close enough to strike, Plaskoe wheeled suddenly, while his Colt Frontier whispered from leather. It spoke with a sharp bark.

Hot agony smashed into Lupe's stomach. He tried to scream, but nothing came out except a gagging sound. Both hands covered the wound and tried to stifle the growing pain. He dropped to his knees and stared hatefully at the *gringo* with the smoking revolver.

"Now goddamnit, that's enough," Plaskoe railed at the bandits. "I own this gun, bought it from a Blue-belly deserter. Ain't no one gonna take it from me."

"Lupe was a friend of ours," one tough bandit growled, hand hovering over the butt of a Spanish imitation of a Colt 1861 Army revolver.

"Yes," several voices rose in chorus.

"I don't like you, *gringo*," a fat bandit named Jose snarled, taking a menacing step forward.

"Do you want a taste of this?" Plaskoe inquired coldly while he swung the muzzle of the .45 in line with the surly bandit's face.

In the distance, El Guillo let out a shrill giggle of delight as he climaxed prematurely.

"The back way. Put it in the back way this time," the little girl begged him.

"I said, do you want to face me with only a *pistola*?" Plaskoe demanded again.

"I . . . uh . . . no. Not at this time. Another time . . . maybe."

"Yeah. In my sleep, no doubt."

"*You call me a coward?*" Jose Bernal could control himself no longer. His fingers closed over the rosewood grips of the percussion pistol and he yanked it free of leather.

Plaskoe's Colt spit fire and drove lead over the short distance. The bullet plowed a deep groove in Jose's right thigh, half an inch from his penis. He howled, dropped his gun and stared horrified at the wound.

"No. I call you a stupid asshole," Plaskoe replied calmly. "Never draw against a man with a gun in his hand. Another inch and we would be calling you Julietta instead of Jose. Listen to me all of you. I've said this before and I want to be sure you understand. *I* own the Gatling gun. Because of it, I have a claim on a large hunk of the loot. Especially the gold. With that gun, El Guillo and the rest of you are unbeatable. Only I know how to work it and clean it and put it back together again. I happen to like making lots of money and I want to live a long time. Anyone, you, or you, or you, Arturo, or anyone else who tries to take it away from me gets killed."

Shelter Morgan had a new bounce in his step—though his knees felt weak and he had been drained dry—as he went along the walk from the boardinghouse where Luisa lived toward the Whaley House. The imposing structure was being used as the county records building and court house. There he expected to find the maps and other documentation on this supposed mine of Tom Plaskoe's. Next to the government ediface, he noticed a sign on another building.

CALIFORNIA MINERS AND
PROSPECTORS ASSOCIATION

Below, in smaller print an inscription that took his

36

immediate attention.

INDEPENDENT MINE OWNERS COUNCIL

That might save a lot of time. On a tall white column of the porch, he saw a smaller placard that displayed an arrow and the word, "OFFICE." Shell followed the direction and entered a small room that gave off of the side of the building, in the space between it and the Whaley House.

"'Afternoon. I'm Shelter Morgan."

"Fine day. Fine day it is, sir," a tall, round-bellied, pink-cheeked fellow bubbled. "The name's Potomus. Mortimer Potomus. I'm president of the Council. What may I do for you?"

"I'm looking for information on the Dorado Mine."

"The Dorado. Ah, yes. Yes, indeed. A remarkable strike. Young feller it was who bought it recently. Old Premus Caulder worked it first. It petered out on him and he looked to unload it on some gullible Easterner. Then this bright-as-a-penny Johnny Reb came along. He bought the Dorado faster'n snappin' your fingers. Ol' Premus felt mighty lucky when he unloaded it on that greenhorn. That is until the boy started pullin' gold out of that number two drift. Premus's fit to be tied now. When he first heard, he off and kicked a stone water trough in Julian so hard it broke a toe." Potomus paused and industriously wiped his small, gold-rimmed spectacles with a clean white handkerchief. His genial disposition darkened a moment.

"Stock's not available in the Dorado Mine, though, Mister Morgan. That Reb never went public with it. Keeps to himself a lot. But, mark you, the success he's had demonstrates the potential in the many mines in the Lagunas. I hold interest in several of them and would be glad to, ah, introduce you to the right persons to make an investment."

"It's too bad about the Dorado," Shell began. He realized

37

that Potomus used this association for an outlet to sell his gold stocks more than a clearing house for the mine owners. He decided to play along.

For ten minutes, Shell asked questions about the other mines, then gradually worked the conversation back to Tom Plaskoe and the Dorado.

"How large an operation is this Dorado?"

"Now mind you, Mister Morgan, the Owners Council only handles his legal matters and banking. That Tom Plaskoe hires two or three men to help him. He needs 'em because he does his own smelting. His output has been growing until now it represents the largest single gold producer, outside the big mining concerns up north. Oh, there's gold in the Lagunas and through the Cuyamacha range. All the more reason why it would be a wise investment to put aside some shares in the public mines there."

"Well now, you see, I've known Tom Plaskoe for a long time. Since during the War. I'm proud to hear of his success, but it leaves me with a problem. I wouldn't feel right puttin' money into another mine instead of my old friend's operation. All the same, I thank you for the time and information," Shell drawled in his best "down home" accent.

"Think nothing of it, Morgan. I've tried to get Tom to incorporate. Talked with him several times. He's stubborn. Now, if you reckon to visit him while you're here, perhaps an old war-buddy could be more persuasive . . ." Rubbing hands eager to share in the riches of the Dorado, Potomus left the offer dangling.

Shell pretended to ponder the idea. "There is that possibility. Yes, I think I might pay good old Tom a short visit. I could . . . appeal to him to be, ah, reasonable."

"Good, good. We see alike on that. If there's anything else I could provide you on Tom's operation, or any other mine in the area, don't hesitate to call on me. Good day, Mister Morgan, and . . . I'll be waiting to hear about your results."

5.

An hour after the day's journey began, the bandit caravan dropped down out of the rugged mountains of Baja California and struck northwestward through the sands of the desert. They would ascend the mountains again, near Jacumba, and thus avoid the army patrols sent out from the cavalry post at Campo, south and east of San Diego. For Tom Plaskoe the hours seemed to drag. He longed to be away from the unfriendly company of the bandidos and once more enjoy some of the luxuries of the port city, with its bright lights and free-flowing champagne. He might even make a gift of his favors to that little Luisa if she treated him nicely enough. Thoughts of the attractive young Mexican whore stirred his loins and he looked over at the girl on the seat beside him.

Maria Elena Montez-Ortega sat in slump-shouldered despair. She had, of course, expected to be raped. Twice during her seventeen years, her village of La Rumorosa had been raided by bandidos, The first time, when she was thirteen, she had been raped by five hard-muscled young men. After the second one, it had actually gotten to be fun. Though, she had to admit, they insisted on being rough and it had hurt her some. This time, only three of El Guillo's men had her, passing her around with almost casual indifference. Maybe a girl eager and willing did not please them. Then the *gringo* with the magical gun had taken an interest in her.

How pathetic he was! His poor little *verga*, stiff as a board, was no bigger than her youngest brother's, and Pepe was only eleven. How hard he jabbed and poked it at her, whining with frustration each time it slipped out, needing only two or three short minutes to release his hot flow and then it would shrivel, not to awaken before at least an hour of hard work on her part. Maria Elena sighed. At least she hadn't been split apart by that *gigante chile* of El Guillo. She had seen it swaying and bobbing in front of him when he had entertained his men by taking the little girl from El Alamo who liked it in her backside. *Como un perro. Muy sucio.* Yes, she thought in reflection, filthy like a dog. She sensed the *gringo* looking intently at her.

"How about it?" Tom Plaskoe panted in his crude Spanish. "I could tie the reins and we could get in the back."

"Right now?" she asked, surprised. "In daylight, in front of all of these men?"

"Why not? They do it in the open all the time, while the others laugh and make bets how long their friends can last. I . . . I'm hard as a rock and I need it bad."

Maria Elena turned her face away so he would not see she was laughing at him. Like a hot little boy on his twelfth birthday, making his first trip to the *putaria* with his father. So desperate, so excited, yet so sad. She lifted her chin and forced a smile as she faced him again.

"All right. Why don't we?"

She climbed over the front wall of the wagon box and ducked low under the gun carriage. Quickly she removed her dress and lay down on it for more comfort. She only hoped he would not explode outside of her again and make more stains. He joined her a moment later, the front of his trousers poking out, body atremble with his agitated eagerness. He freed his organ of clothing and dropped to his knees between her wide-spread thighs. He kept his eyes rapturously fixed on her bronze-covered, hairless mound that spread wide to expose delicately pink and orangish-red folds, like a giant sea muscle.

Plaskoe's mouth watered and he longed to plunge his tongue into that wetly glistening crease and partake of the most delightful of forbidden feasts. Her lack of hair excited him wildly. His cock throbbed and his balls ached. She made him think of those little gals he had diddled back in Tennessee before the War.

He was sixteen then and the only ones who could get him worked up were the girls who hadn't grown old enough to develop a thatch over their puffy mounds. Up in those isolated Tennessee hills, he had to content himself with some cousins, two younger sisters and the three little girls who lived down the road. Most of them had said he had the biggest pecker they had ever seen and that made him feel good. They all fitted him tightly and brought him the only real satisfaction he had known in all his life. Now, things were different for him. The little ones were out. The others made fun often as not. At least, though, he had Maria Elena. With a sob of anguished pleasure, he buried his face between her thighs, grown sweaty from the hot desert sun.

"*Oye!* The *gringo* is getting a little lunch," one bandit called to his friends.

"Twenty pesos says he goes off within two minutes like a shotgun," another wagered.

"If he does, tell him not to make a mess on that magical gun," El Guillo roared through his laughter.

"Before anything else," her mother had told her, "stay alive." In the seven years since that first mother-daughter talk about men and passion and the possibility of rape for a poor girl in a remote village, Maria Elena had kept that wisdom uppermost in her heart. She might have been a little free with her treasures, but she wasn't a *puta*. Ever since her capture she had striven to please with the gifts of her body in order to stay alive. Mostly, without any involvement of love or romance, it had been boring and uncomfortable. Even with the tiny member of the *gringo*. Only now . . . now something more marvelous than anything she had experienced in seventeen years had begun to happen to her and she . . . she LOVED IT! She twined her fingers in his strange, white hair and shoved his head down against her tingling, wildly stimulated cleft.

"Aaaah! Tomas, Tomas . . . more! Do it more! I love it, love

41

it!'' she shrieked into the dry desert air.

After the heights of ecstacy his tongue had brought her to, Maria Elena wanted to cry with frustration at the fumbling, prodding attempt her Tomas made at entering her with his verga. Their ungainly coupling continued until the caravan began to ascend the hills once more and the column reached a crossroads where El Guillo deemed it safe to part company and let the gringo go on into his own country. Tomas made one final, valiant effort, thrust hard three times and reached release with a shudder and a whimper. He parted from her and drew up his trousers.

"You all lose," El Guillo chuckled to his companions. "He outlasted himself by many hours. Perhaps you should have a carreta for your bed, amigo?" he teased Plaskoe. "Here we must part. Hurry and dispose of our gold, then bring our share to the next meeting place. You know where."

"Yes. It will take nine or ten days," Plaskoe informed the bandit leader.

"Take two weeks," El Guillo offered magnanimously. "Now, adios."

"Good-bye to you, Rudy."

"*Chingado*," El Guillo snarled. "Always the rude little name."

"Sorry."

"Never mind. You will never change, gringo."

"I . . . ah, have something for you to put in safe keeping for me," Plaskoe told the outlaw chief.

"Eh? What is this?"

Plaskoe bent down and raised Maria Elena to her feet. "Keep an eye on her for me, will you?" He winked in a manly confidence. "If you want to sample the goods, I'll assure you they are of prime quality."

"*Gracias, amigo.* I shall see she receives all that she needs."

In a drumroll of hoofs, the bandidos whirled and rode away,

42

south. Tom Plaskoe looked northwest, to the sawtoothed ridge of the Laguna Mountains. Behind them, he knew, lay the Cuyamacha Peaks and the road to his mine. Whistling contentedly, he entertained himself with visions of his delightful afternoon with Maria Elena, the best he'd had since boyhood, while he dismantled and carefully hid away the Gatling gun.

Potomus gave out more information than Morgan could use. "I haven't seen Tom in nearly four months. He usually comes out of the hills with a load of ingots about every three or so. Figure he'll be in any time now. He showed up here shortly after the war. Didn't look to have two cents to rub together. Then he up and buys that mine. Weren't no time until the gold started rolling out."

"He brings his gold all the way here?"

"Nope. Just to Julian. The Banner Queen Mine is operating there. They make a joint shipment to me here, on armed wagons with mounted escort. It'd be foolish to do anything else. There's bandits in those hills. White, Mex and Indian. Once he consigns the gold to the shippers in Julian, he heads on here for a celebration while his workers pick up supplies and dynamite. Sometimes, like in the winter, he don't even leave the mountain. He spends time drinking and partaking of the ladies at the Blue Lantern Sporting House in Julian, then heads back to the mine."

"You'd mentioned workers before. How many does he have?"

"Last time I heard, it was three." The mine broker frowned slightly. "Can't say I entirely approve of his choices. They're drifters and gunslicks the lot of 'em if you ask me."

"After he takes a draft for entertainment here in town, how much money, actually, do you usually send to his bank in Julian?"

"Well now," Potomus hedged, "that's mighty confidential information. Are you tellin' me straight that you're a friend of

43

his? I wouldn't want to violate our relationship by blabbin' to any high-binder who walked in off the street."

"My word of honor as an officer and gentleman of the Confederacy, suh," Shell returned solemnly. "I've known Tom Plaskoe for years. We served in the same regiment."

"Well, then, well . . . I suppose . . ." The Mine Owners Council president cleared his throat behind a pudgy hand that had never seen a pick handle, then went on in a near whispered rush. "He instructed me to send no less than two thirds of his funds back to Julian. Sometimes all of it if he isn't staying here more than over night."

"What would he do with it there?"

"Beats me. That's it, all the same."

"All I need to know is how to find the mine."

Potomus' eyes grew shifty. "If you promise, really give your oath, not to tell where it came from, I'll provide you with a map of the hills, marking the location of Tom's mine."

"I appreciate that. I swear not to reveal any of our conversation, even to Tom."

"That's fine with me. Now, here, let me show you."

Darkness lay heavily over the Laguna Mountains and hunting owls swooped low among the pines. Their mournful hoots accompanied Tom Plaskoe to the narrow, brush-choked lane that led to his mine. He shivered slightly in the chill mountain air, following a day on the desert, and hunched his shoulders to conserve warmth. He had taken time to grease the carreta's axles and the ear-shredding shriek no longer kept pace with his progress.

A mile and a half of the constricted path snaked around the belly of one mount, to end at last in a small clearing in the pines. As the tall, solid wooden wheels ground smaller chunks of decomposed granite into powder, a darker shadow detached itself from the blackness of a low shelter and raised a rifle.

"It's me, Struthers. We've got a whole lot to unload. The

rest is in the cache on the other side of the border. You an'
Dave go after it tomorrow, drive the wagons back here."

"Good to see ya, Boss."

"There . . . there been anybody around?"

"Nope. Not a soul. Seen a big brown bear the other day.
Took a shot at it, but the bastard got away. Bagged a couple of
them Injuns' sheep, though, so we got lots of good eats."

"Gawk! Those ancient hulks. They taste like boot polish."

Two more men came from the brush-roofed sleeping
quarters and began to unload sections of the Gatling gun. By
shielded lantern light they looked over the mounds of gold coin
and religious articles hidden in burlap bags.

"Sure wish you'd brought along some o' them cuddly
Mezkin gals," Dave observed.

"A lot of good they would have done you, Dave," Mike
Struthers told his partner in crime. "First thing in the mornin'
we're off to get the rest of the loot. You try an' fuck all night
an' you'd be worse than wet noodles for doin' hard work."

"Bet me. I'm horny as a three-peckered billy goat and ram
enough to use all three."

"In a pig's ass," the youngest hardcase piped up in a voice
still not settled down from adolescence.

"In your ass, Sammy, if I don't get to town soon."

"You can forget that," pimply-faced Sammy Grimes
snapped. "You take a try at me an' I'll give you a new belly
button."

"Yeah," Mike Struthers snickered. "Thirty-six caliber
size."

Defensive about the small weapon he carried, Sammy
flushed red and fired back. "I got small hands. I can't help it."

"Keep it down, all of you," Tom Plaskoe warned.

"What's the matter, Boss?"

"I . . . don't know. Something preyin' on me."

Through his long journey from the border to the mine, Tom
Plaskoe had felt uneasy, as though he might be watched. If
someone had followed him, he could be out there now, watch-

ing and listening. It made him decidedly nervous. At first he had seen the mine as a clever way to convert his share of the stolen gold into usable cash. When it ran low, a fortunate circumstance brought him to meet Master Sergeant Blake Manning. Manning, a quartermaster sergeant, had been dipping into Army funds. When the army found out, he took it on the run. For added insurance, he brought along a Gatling gun and enough ammunition to refight the Battle of Shiloh.

Pleased with the prospect of owning the rapid-firing weapon, Plaskoe struck a bargain, arranged a meeting place and paid a huge sum to the credulous sergeant and took delivery of the powerful Gatling gun he presently used in his raids in Baja. Immediately after the transaction, Plaskoe shot Manning to death and buried him in the vastness of the Arizona desert. His return to the mine marked a beginning.

Not until he met Rudolfo Santacruz did his scheme come to fruition. With the Gatling gun he was able to participate with the bandits and yet not be murdered for his share or simply because he was a gringo. The scheme had lasted a long time. Sooner or later, he knew, someone would realize that things weren't as they seemed. Too much gold, perhaps, at one time. Or for a long while after all the other claims had run dry. Someone could pull an assay of his ingots and discover they contained a high quality of base metal, as did any workable gold for chalices or coins. He realized he could not keep that day off forever. However, if he had been followed, the whole project could be in jeopardy. He made a conscious effort to shake off the feeling of pending doom. They had to get the gold down into the lower level tunnel where his small smelter had been erected and make ready to reduce it to ingots. Once the other wagon loads had been safely brought in he would work quickly so he could head to Julian and then return to Mexico.

Maybe one more big haul would see him financially fixed for life.

6.

When the sun creeped over Presidio Hill and shed brightness on the solid adobe buildings of Old Town and Alonso Horton's New Town, San Diego began to come to life. Shelter Morgan went to Wayland's Stables and checked on his horse, then sought out the owner of the livery.

"I need a sturdy pack mule," he informed the stooped, gray-haired man.

"In this country, burros would do you better. They can go a lot longer without water."

"Do you have any?"

"Yep. Rent or buy?"

"Depends on the price."

The liveryman's eyes glowed. He loved to dicker with the same pleasure as his counterpart, Gabriel Bandini, down in Old Town. "You take a look at 'em and then we can talk money."

"I have to gather some supplies first. Then I'll have some idea of how many I might need."

Another glow of interest sparked in Wayland's eyes. He might unload a whole string on this greenhorn. "Fine. You do that. I'll be here all day."

Shell got a quick breakfast first, biscuits, eggs and some cheese and onions rolled in cornmeal pancakes, called *enchiladas*. Then he located a general mercantile.

"I'll want two of those canvas water bags, big ones. Two hundred rounds of forty-four-forty, a hundred of forty-five." Shelter had recently become familiar with the Colt Army Model 73 revolver in .45 caliber and came to like it. Following

47

an unusual stint with the Fifth Infantry, he had purchased a civilian version, called the "Frontier Model 74." It had a great deal besides lighter weight to recommend it over his old cap-and-ball Walker Colt.

"You got your own cookin' gear?" a pinched-faced, bespectacled clerk inquired. "If you're headin' out in the mountains, cafes are few and far between."

"Uh . . . no. What do you recommend?"

"A dutch oven, skillet, granite coffee pot, long-handle spoon and fork, tin plate, maybe a stew pot. You'll need a tripod or trestle for your cookfire. We've got the whole caboodle so's it will fit in this here tucker box. It carries right nice on a pack-saddle. The slant side opens out so you can get to your stuff and the inner surface can be used as a cuttin' board to slice meat or fillet a fish. There's compartments, too, for flour, beans, that sort of thing."

This search was starting to cost him a lot. Shell appreciated the extra money he had acquired from collecting a few bounties along the way. "I'll take the whole thing. Fix it up with everything you listed, some salt, too, and a pound of coffee beans and a mill. I'll need some blankets as well, two should do it."

For the first time, the clerk brightened. "Yes, sir. Right away. Now, them Mezkin blankets is the best. All wool and mighty warm for nights in the mountains." Shell nodded and the clerk added the bill. "That'll be twenty-two dollars and thirty-seven cents."

Shell paid him. "I'll be back to pick it up when I have my pack animal."

Walking back down India Street, Shell considered the task ahead of him. He had no idea how long it would take to corner Plaskoe. An odd suspicion niggled in the back of his mind. The amount of gold that Potomus reported being taken out of the mine far exceeded what Plaskoe would have received as his share of the stolen Confederate booty. Plaskoe had been selling ingots for far too long since the end of the war. When he had started his self-appointed task of hunting down the murderers and thieves who had taken the gold from him and his men, Shelter Morgan had been at a great disadvantage.

Seven years in a Yankee prison had made the trail dim at best, invisible in most places. He had gone to the authorities with his story. It met with indifference everywhere, often with outright hostility.

"Who cares about Rebels stealing Rebel gold? The war is over, Mister Morgan," an under-secretary in the War Department told him. "You were an officer, albeit a Secessionist and a Rebel, you ought to know that in war many awful things happen that would be considered criminal under normal circumstances. Forget it, that's my advice."

Shell hadn't forgotten. Met with rebuffs at all levels, he set out on his own. He had relied on rumors, messages from friends who knew of his search, sometimes an article in a newspaper. Many of the men had long since spent their share by the time Shelter tracked them down. He doubted that Plaskoe would have been an exception. He also suspected that Plaskoe was not the type to undertake the back-breaking labor of mining to obtain it. Where, then, did he get this large and continuous supply of gold? Obviously he had to find it somewhere. To learn that would take a long while. Morgan had every intention of finding out.

Pure, crystal air at four thousand feet gave the sun a particular brightness in the early morning while Tom Plaskoe and his three henchmen loaded an ore wagon with the cooled ingots of gold. The few jewels he had removed from their settings in chalices and rings, he carried in a soft leather pouch around his neck. Those he would sell to a jeweler he knew in San Diego who asked no questions and paid fair prices. Since he trusted Sammy Grimes and the others no more than he did El Guillo, he had long ago made special preparations.

A false bottom had been built into the forward portion of the

49

wagon box. There he placed his powerful Gatling gun and closed the lid on it. If he left it behind, he had no doubts that it would be gone, along with his workers, on his return. Over that he stacked the first layers of gold. The feeling of being hunted, even after three days, had not dissipated and he carefully studied the land around the mine. Someone, a tiny voice whispered in his mind, had come looking for him. He forced the premonition from his consciousness and stood by while his men put the remaining converted loot into the ore wagon.

"Sammy, it's your turn to come with me to Julian. Spend no more than one night there, then bring the wagon and supplies back to the mine."

"Yes, sir, Boss," the adenoidal young gunslick croaked. He had visions of a big steak, some fresh vegetables, a lot of beer and maybe . . . maybe . . . He'd best push that thought away before it showed below his belt, Sammy thought fiercely.

"I ordered a half-hog for this trip," Plaskoe announced. "You boys can build a pit and roast it. Have a real feed for once."

"That's mighty nice of you," they chorused.

"Time to go, Sammy," Plaskoe said as he mounted the driver's seat.

As they rode along through the live oaks and pines, Tom Plaskoe's mind wandered back over the years to the start of it all. He wondered what had happened to all those good ol' boys who had shared in the quarter-million in gold. He had heard that General Custis had killed himself. Foolish thing to do. Colonel Fainer was dead, too. As was Major Twyner and his useless kid brother. Someone had killed them all. He hadn't heard who, but the thought chilled him and he considered again the strange feeling that someone had followed him to the mine and even now watched him. Could it be the man? Who and why?

Jeb Thornton was dead, Welton Williams, too. Every one of the boys guarding that gold had died, even Captain Morgan. Leastwise, they were never seen again. Only Dink Dinkum and the captain had ridden out of that small clearing. Wounded, both of them. The Yankees got 'em most likely, if they didn't leak to death from bullet holes. Why, then, should he feel so uncomfortable? Sammy wanted to make small talk and Plaskoe let it run in one ear and out the other side while the wheels ground over the narrow road through the Cuayamachas toward Julian.

Shelter Morgan rode out of San Diego on the stage road. He would pass through an area that some people had recently begun to call Spring Valley, then on to a vast Mexican Grant rancho, Rancho Jamul, Portrero and at last to Campo, short of High Pass and the saw-tooth, barren ridges of the Laguna Mountains. A small cavalry post was located at Campo and it would be there that his instructions said to turn north through a wide valley that would lead him to the western slopes of the Cuayamachas. Eventually he would reach Julian. Shelter wanted to visit the small mining village to learn what he could about Tom Plaskoe before starting out to the mine. His journey proved a pleasant one.

The terrain was pristine, the trees smelled sweet and clean. Cattle, sheep and goats grazed in profusion, watched by bare-foot, shirtless brown boys wearing straw sombreros. Most of the youngsters were Mexican, or Mexican and Indian mixed, though here and there he saw a flash of yellow-white hair and candid blue eyes gazing thoughtfully at him as he rode along. All of them were deeply colored by the sun and jabbered with each other in a mixture of Spanish and English. They lived and worked, as did their parents, on the big ranchos, most of which were now owned by white men. The relaxing, pastoral scene lulled Morgan into easing his usually taut control. He made Campo the first night and camped there within the sound of bugle calls from the small military post.

It made him think of his recent adventure when he searched for Rory Simmons, a particularly nasty individual who had aided in stealing the gold. His pursuit took him into the ranks of the Fifth United States Infantry. The golden notes of the bugle at retreat formation, announcing the evening meal and taps, brought a warm glow of nostalgia to Morgan's chest. By the time he set out the next morning, he had nearly let down his guard completely.

Four men suddenly appeared on the trail through the valley. They wore huge sombreros, trimmed in silver, with gaudy trousers and jackets, dripping silver conchos. Their shirts, though fancy and frilly, had discolored to a dismal gray and showed food stains. The one on the far left peeled off and rode into the trees while the remaining three proceeded down the trail to where Shell had reined in. Wise in the ways of the frontier and well trained from his days with the Confederate Army, Shell instantly suspected a trap.

Why would they seek to rob him? he wondered. Or could they be after someone else? As they approached, the apparent leader smiled broadly under his arched, hawk nose, revealing yellowed, crooked teeth. A brace of ancient pistols protruded from a wide red sash tied around his waist. Less than five feet separated them when the dark-skinned man and his companions reined in. He raised his empty right hand, palm out in a sign of peaceful intent.

"*Ay, buenas dias, amigo,*" he greeted with much affability. "It is good to see a friendly face along this lonely trail. I am called Raul Manuel Sanchez."

"M'name's Shelter Morgan."

"*Con mucho gusto.* What brings you to this so beautiful place? Are you, by chance a miner? A gold miner?" Sanchez inquired, with a light of avarice in his small, close-set black eyes. His spreading belly hung over the large, Mexican style saddle horn and swelled upward nearly to his chest. He dug a thick finger into one ear and took breath to speak again.

"A friend of mine, who was in San Diego only a day ago, has told me of a fine *gringo* who matches your description. It was said that you would be riding this way. My *amigos* and I

52

thought to welcome you. According to talk in town, this *caballero* is supposed to be a friend of Tomas Plaskoe, the man with the so successful gold mine that turns out ingots like water from a spring. It occurred to us . . . only in passing, you see . . . that surely a friend of the *rico gringo*, Plaskoe, would have to also be very wealthy. Consider the handsome blooded horse, the sturdy burro packed with many goods. Who knows what else such a one might bring into our mountains?"

"That's true enough," Shell replied. He decided to play along for a while. He wanted to know what the local riff-raff might think about Plaskoe. "Yes, your informant gave you an accurate description. I am the friend of Tom Plaskoe he mentioned. I knew him during the recent War."

"Ah! The war between your states, *verdad*? Such an unpleasant conflict. All that violence. It is a bad thing, violence, no? Much better that people be *amigos* and not make war." His eyes gazed beyond Morgan, as though looking for something . . . or someone.

Shelter worked his Remington derringer down his sleeve from the small holster given him by a gambler in Dodge City, Kansas. All the while he continued to smile and make small talk.

"Absolutely. I have always been a man of peace."

"That takes great self-control, *Señor*."

"It does. One thing I have observed, though," Shelter went on as he palmed the over-and-under barreled .41 rim-fire pop-gun, "is that *amigos* don't often stall for time, as though waiting for someone to get into a position to jump their friends from behind."

With a smooth, swift move, Morgan whipped around in the saddle, while cocking the derringer's hammer. He lined the barrels on the chest of a bandido no more than six feet away on a boulder under a large oak tree. In the taut instant of silence, birdsong filled the valley until the Remington cracked loudly.

The small, underpowered bullet struck the bandit in his chest. It didn't penetrate the sternum, though, but disrupted

53

his plans with a jolt of severe pain that caused him to topple off the ragged hunk of granite and strike his head against a smaller stone. He lay there unconscious.

Reversing his movement, Shell swung around while his right hand dipped to his holster and drew his Colt Frontier .45.

A big two hundred fifty grain slug smashed into the chest of the outlaw on Sanchez's right and drove him from the saddle, his heart burst by the expanding lead. With considerable alacrity, and no consideration for the demands of *macho*, the man on the other side wheeled his horse and rode away at a frantic gallop as though pursued by the hounds of Hell. That left the two weapons in Shell's hands pointed directly at the protruding belly of Raul Sanchez.

Sanchez, who styled himself as *El Tiburon*, the Shark, had barely been able to free the pair of Model 1808 Navy flintlock pistols from his sash. Although faced with deadly force, he had presence enough to manage a blush and produced a foolish grin that twisted his thick lips.

"I seem to be outclassed, *amigo*," he managed in a low voice, devoid of his previous bravado.

"Yes, violence *is* a terrible thing, is it not, *amigo*?" Morgan asked dryly.

7.

Slowly Sanchez lowered his arms and let the antique pistols drop gently to the soft turf. He nodded toward Morgan, who kept his own weapons centered on the expanse of gut in front of him.

"You ought to have a better choice in weapons if you want to be an outlaw," Morgan observed.

Sanchez shrugged. "I am only, ah, beginning the exciting life of a highwayman, *Señor*. You see how that is?"

"Your story interests me, Sanchez. Tell me more."

"My friends call me *El Tiburon*, the Shark. My enemies call me *El Bastardo* because my father used my mother without benefit of the church and then simply left." The chubby, young-faced bandit shrugged in a typical Mexican gesture. "From that encounter, I came along nine months later. I have had a hard life, *Señor* Morgan, as you can imagine. I ran away from home at eleven. I joined up with a bandido gang run by a man who calls himself El Guillo. I did odd work around the camp, cared for the horses. Some of the men used me badly, in a manner I will not remark on, but I grew older. I was quick and strong and I could use my fists. They found other interests. At last El Guillo gave me a gun and let me ride with them. Four years ago, for no reason I could understand, El Guillo threw me out of the gang. I have had to make do as I could since then."

Sanchez looked at the dead man and the unconscious one sprawled on the ground. "Perhaps I should have made a better choice of men to follow me."

"Perhaps you should have made a better choice of victims,"

Shell amended dryly. "Something makes me like you, Raul. Somehow you seem to be a nice enough sort of fellow. Have you been in these mountains long?"

"Oh, *si*. Since El Guillo chased me out."

"Maybe you could tell me a little about my old war buddy, Plaskoe."

"I would be happy to oblige, *Señor*. What is it that the brave and daring *Americano* wishes to know?"

Morgan quickly formed his line of questioning. "Well, old Tom sometimes had a habit of wandering off and coming by money in what some folks might call the easy way. Now, as it happens, you appear to be in a line of work that might appeal to Tom. Have you ever happened to have dealings with him? Or know anyone who has?"

Sanchez frowned slightly and thought it over. "No. I know nothing of this rich miner being involved in anything of that nature. With all that gold, what would be his need? There is El Guillo, whom I mentioned a moment ago. He is a powerful *bandido*. He and his men wander the length and breadth of Baja California Frontera, taking from the poor as readily as from the rich. If any such temptations came to *Señor* Plaskoe, surely El Guillo would know of it.

"Since I left his band, El Guillo is said to have come by enormous firepower. Some people claim a *gringo* rides with El Guillo, though that is hard to believe. Your people are not well-liked in Mexico," he explained apologetically. "Men who would ride with *bandidos* even less. One thing that might be of interest to you, though it is most likely only coincidence."

"Go on."

"It seems that not long after word comes that El Guillo has taken an exceptionally large amount of loot from villages and churches, Plaskoe soon makes another shipment of gold. That doesn't mean anything, of course. Though there has been loose talk around Ramona and Julian about how Plaskoe seems to pull an enormous amount of gold out of the ground. Also, when El Guillo's men visit Tecate to enjoy themselves, they seem to have a lot of *gringo* dollars, though they raid only in Baja California. Perhaps Plaskoe is buying their haul and melting that down."

"That might be worth looking into. Now, I want you to ease that old rifle out of its scabbard and let 'er slide to the ground. Then back your horse about ten steps."

After Sanchez complied, Morgan dismounted and gathered up the weapons of the dead man and his unconscious companion. He added these to El Tiburon's contribution and lashed them together in a tarpaulin on one side of the pack-saddle.

"You know, Raul, you really should look into some other line of work."

"Alas," El Tiburon replied as he shrugged and made a two-handed, palms up gesture, "I have been told that this is the line my father was in."

Morgan spurred his mount off in the direction taken by the fleeing would-be highwayman. The trail led toward Julian. Shelter reached the small village two hours before sundown. He decided to forget about the bandit. He probably knew less than Sanchez. He took his horse and burro to the livery and saw them bedded down for the night, then strolled to the Julian Hotel and paid for a room. The sun lingered in a rosy glow over the low western peaks when he sat down to a dinner of bear steak, boiled potatoes and cabbage with apple cobbler for dessert.

Tired and ready for the comfort of a real bed, he went back to his small cubical and fell almost instantly into a deep, restful sleep. An hour later, a loud knocking on the ill-fitted door awakened him.

"Who is it?" Shell came out of the bed, Colt in his hand, and tiptoed on bare feet to the side of the door.

"Open up!" came an accented voice. "*Andele, amigo.*"

Muzzle held at stomach level, Shell turned the knob and

57

jerked open the portal.

There stood Raul Sanchez, complete with a new set of weapons. *"Amigo!"* he cried. "You must let me show you Julian."

Morgan groaned through a grin. So unlikely a bandit could not help but be liked. "Come on in."

"Thank you, my frien'. This town she is not so much, but there are sights to see all the same. I wan' to let you be my guest and to enjoy a night of friendly drinking, good music and pretty women. You will come, no?"

"I'm tired, Raul. I thought I left you on the trail."

"Oh, *si*, but a fellow happened along who had little caution for his safety and less use for these fine revolvers. I, ah, persuaded him to make a gift of them so that I might come here in proper style and join forces with you, my frien'. It came to me that perhaps you are not so much a frien' to Tom Plaskoe as you told me. In that case, why so many questions? *Porque no*, the answer is simplicity itself. You plan to rob him, *verdad*?"

"Not . . . exactly." For no reason he could explain, perhaps through years of habit, Morgan felt compelled to explain to Raul. "He is the one who robbed me. Long years ago. I wish only to return the favor for him and see that the men who died trying to protect a shipment of gold are avenged."

"Ah-ha! *Venganza*. That is a motive I can understand. *Muy macho*. So, it is the two of us who will do this thing. First, though, you must see Raquel, Simone, Bebe Angelica and Rita. They are beautiful, you will agree. There is also the *china*, Mai-Ling. Also we must drink to our partnership with some good tequila. We are lucky for each other my frien', in four years I have not made such a haul as the one today. And after you had taken my weapons too. Come, come, get your clothes on."

"I'm not so sure about this partnership."

"You wound me, *amigo*. Here I ride into this town at great risk to offer my valuable services and you will say no. How is that? Where is your gratitude for me sparing you out on the trail this morning?"

58

"You . . . spared . . . me? Somehow I saw that in a different light."

"*Como si, como no.* It is one in the same, is it not? Hurry. The good times are waiting."

Chuckling again, Shelter Morgan shrugged into his trousers, put on boots and gunbelt and the two men started for the door.

Yellow light spilled from kerosene lamps that illuminated the interiors of Julian's three saloons. Raul steered Morgan past the first and settled for the next in line.

Here the lights were lower, the sawdust on the floor dirtier and the women coarser. Raul seemed to like it well enough. He waved an arm expansively and called for tequila. His black eyes swiveled in their sockets and recorded all of the soiled doves in the establishment. The two he settled on seemed far from thrilled at the honor.

"He's here again. I'll toss you for it, Lavinia," one fallen lady offered.

"Sure." The second girl produced a coin and flipped it.

"Heads," the first hooker declared.

"It's tails, Marge," her sister in sin announced. "You lose. That means you have that mighty bandido of the backcountry, El Tiburon."

"I'm oh so thrilled," Marge grumbled.

Together, they sauntered toward the table where Raul and Shelter sat with their drinks. Marge took a chair beside Raul, while Lavinia curled herself into Morgan's lap.

"Listen, everybody," Raul called in a loud voice. "I want you to know that this is *Señor* Shelter Morgan. He is my closest *amigo* and my new partner. He is to be feared and respected the same as El Tiburon."

A quick glance clearly showed Morgan that the announcement had immediately lost him a lot of respect among the locals. Even so, Lavinia didn't seem to mind. She nuzzled her soft lips against his throat and one inquisitive hand groped in his crotch until the former Rebel captain's weapon had grown to cannon-size. A little bit more of that and he would be in a visibly embarrassing position. While he tried to curb her enthusiasm, the barkeep brought the girls drinks without being asked.

"Put it on my tab," El Tiburon grandly commanded.

"My, you're a big . . . big man," Lavinia murmured in Shelter's ear, measuring his stiffened rod at better than a double hand-span. "Would you like to go up to my room? We could look into . . . this a little further." She gave his throbbing organ a playful tweak.

"Go ahead, *amigo*, it is on me," Raul confided with a leer and a wink.

With an offer like that, why not? Shelter didn't like paying for his pleasure and rarely ever did. Usually he managed to obtain all he desired without crass considerations. Besides, he was curious. What sort of a performance would Lavinia put in, considering this remote mountain village? He eased the lady of the night from his lap and started to stand.

"*Ay!* Hurry up, Margarita," Raul cried to the girl beside him. "Let us go upstairs also. My *chile* is so hard it is like a hot slab of rock."

"Are you really his new partner?" Lavinia inquired of Shell once they had entered the narrow crib she called a room.

"*He* thinks so."

"Ha! Like I thought. He's not a . . . very good outlaw. Are you?"

"I'm not an outlaw at all."

"Then what . . . I'm sorry. I should never ask." Humming tunelessly, she removed her few garments, revealing a lusher and younger body than Shelter had expected. He felt an increase of tension in his loins and hurried to disrobe.

"Oh, my yes," Lavinia exclaimed. "Such a *big* man."

She reached out and started to stroke Shelter's engorged shaft. "Ummh. Maybe I had better use two hands."

"That's nice," Shelter murmured when she closed both of her soft hands around his length and soothingly exercised it.

She watched his phallus raptly for a long moment, then sank

60

to her knees. Her rich auburn hair cascaded over her shoulders as she leaned forward. Her sea-green eyes made a shy glance up at his face a moment before her tongue darted out and circled the sensitive tip of his flaming wand. The little shivers began again. Once more she circled it, then nibbled her way along the shaft to its thick base. She kissed the firm, pulsing sack suspended below, then turned her attention back to his turgid lance.

"Anyone . . . ever . . . take you . . . all the way . . . in?" she inquired between licks.

"Only once," Shell responded, thinking a brief moment of Luisa.

"Well, then, we'll have to make up for lost chances."

Lavinia gulped him, throat and lips working in churning effort as she pulled his enormous mass deep within her moist, warm throat. Shelter swayed and involuntarily thrust his hips forward. Lavinia gulped and accommodated more of his maleness. She seemed tireless. When at last her nose nuzzled in his bristly thatch, Shell poised on the edge of a mighty explosion. Swiftly she withdrew her attentions, leaving him in a tingling limbo.

She pressed one of his hands to her slickly flowing cleft as she came to her feet. "Now's the time. Take me, you big, wonderful man."

Instead of the sagging bed, Lavinia hopped up on a high table and spread her legs wide. "Walk up on it, sweetie," she cooed.

Feeling his need as a pounding demand, he readily complied.

When he neared, she reached out to guide him, inserting the dark red tip in her slippery divide and wetting it well before allowing it to spread wide the outer portals and plunge into her silken passage. Her eyes widened and she uttered a short groan as his vastness enlarged her canal with a rending sensation.

Tight rings rubbed his bulk as Shell pressed forward. The solid grasp on his member gave way only slowly as he took a half-step, then another. A third was required before he had sunk his entire shaft into the pit. Lavinia locked her legs around his hips and sighed contentedly. Happiness swirled in her head and her gaze grew glassy.

"This . . . is . . . like . . . my . . . very first . . . time," she panted in rhythm to his bold, powerful thrusts that drove that rigid machine deep within her being. "I love it like this. Do it! Oh, do it more!"

Time blended for them both and only a few strains from the tinkling piano below reached past Shell's ears as he churned away in that slippery purse. Lavinia threw her head from side to side and a squeal of delight came from deep in her chest when she let go of her professional calm and surrendered to the horny little girl deep within her. Her breasts, medium in size, jiggled with their exertions and their rosy nipples stood up in rigid attention.

Shell grasped her buttocks with one hand, used the other to tease those swaying orbs to greater sensitivity. At last he felt himself building and speeded the gyrating plunges of his hips until he took flight and expended himself.

There's no such thing as a bad lay, he consoled himself as they changed positions and cuddled on the bed. At least Lavinia proved not to be rabbit-fast. Once was definitely not going to be enough for her. Slowly she rekindled the fires in his groin and he felt his flesh warm and expand. She teased it to fullness and then wriggled into position facing him. Somehow it seemed a bit too sordid to Morgan. He managed to maintain a fine erection though as it slid deeply into her flowing passage. More than an hour went by before she ceased inventing new ways for them to couple. Quickly she rose from the bed and began to dress.

"That's all. I'll get in trouble if we're up here too long."

Somehow that didn't seem to ring true to Shell. He shrugged and dressed. Downstairs, he had made it halfway to the door when the bartender hurried up.

"You forgetting something, bandido," he asked with a sneer.

"Not that I know of."

"That tab. Your partner told me you would settle for everything. Now cough it up or I'll get the constable."

Oh no! A sudden suspicion grew into a certainty in Shell's mind. He'd been had in the worst sort of way. He hurriedly paid the bill and left the saloon. He knew only too well what he might expect.

Back at the hotel, he climbed the stairs two at a time. The door to his room stood open a crack. Suddenly cautious, he drew his six-gun and approached with worry furrowing his brow. An ambush?

No. His fast kick and dive into the room revealed it to be empty. No lurking El Tiburon, no packsaddle, camp gear, blankets or rifle. Cleaned out entirely. A scrap of white on the washstand caught his attention.

"El Tiburon wins one way or another! Viva El Tiburon!" the note triumphantly declared.

Robbed and rolled like a beardless boy. Hot anger burst to flame in Shelter Morgan's breast.

8.

Shelter Morgan stared at the note. Anger and disgust mingled in his sour expression. Not a hell of lot could be done that night, he reasoned. Sanchez would be far away by now. He undressed and spent a restless hour slowly falling asleep.

By morning, word of his debacle had preceded him through town. The villagers showed him little sympathy. Some laughed at him, though not to his face, which wore a dark, thunderous expression. He stopped in at the saloon he had visited with Sanchez the night before. When he asked for any information on Raul Sanchez, the bartender replied in scorn.

"Why'd you take up with garbage like that in the first place?"

"I want to talk with that girl, Marge, that he was with last night."

"She's asleep."

"Wake her."

The barkeep started to protest, then thought better of it when he looked closely at Shell's face. He left the bar and climbed to the second floor. Five minutes later, a yawning Marge came down the stairs.

"Funniest way I ever made my fee," she told Morgan when he questioned her. "Never even had his tallywhacker up. He just paid me and climbed out the window. Told me to stay put for an hour or so and dropped to the ground. I didn't have any idea what he was up to."

"Do you know where he might go?"

"Well . . ." She screwed her face into a look of concentration. "He's been here a few times. Seems he once let slip he had a camp west of here, over on the desert slope of the Lagunas."

"Thank you, Marge. I'll find him."

"That's a lot of ground to cover," she cautioned Morgan.

"I've got a lot of reason to catch up to him."

"You do, you cut his balls off," the bartender growled.

For the first time that morning, Shelter smiled. "Reckon I just might do that."

At the livery, a grizzled old prospector stood jawing with the stablehand. He paused to study Morgan when he entered. Then he stepped forward and extended a hard hand.

"Name's Wilson, friends call me George. Hear you ran afoul of Raul Sanchez."

"That's right," Shelter returned in a flat tone.

"You fixin' to hunt him down?"

"Could be."

"You'd do a mite better with somethin' besides that six-shooter. It just happens I've got me a spare Winchester I've a mind to loan out. A saddle, too."

"That's . . . that's mighty nice of you, George. I'd make certain to get them back to you at the earliest chance. My name is Shelter Morgan."

"I'd heard that already, Shelter. You strike me as a reasonable man." A cackle of laughter followed. "That little bastard has done something like what he pulled on you to nearly everyone in town at one time or another. They gave you short shrift 'cause they're too embarrassed to admit to it. It does their mean little hearts good to see someone else taken for a change."

"People are . . . pretty much the same anywhere, I suppose," Shell answered philosophically. "I do thank you for the loan. I'll take my horse and be on my way."

"If I was you, I wouldn't go lookin' for him over toward the desert. Strike off along the Cuyamacha trail that leads back to the San Diego stage road. Whenever ol' Tiburon makes another score, he likes to sidle down to Tecate and brag it up a bit among the Mezkins. Makes him feel like a real bandido."

"Much obliged," Shell offered.

A quarter of an hour later, Shelter rode out of town, taking the road recommended by George Wilson. He hadn't gone far before he recognized a familiar hoofprint. He dismounted and studied it. For sure, it belonged to the horse ridden by Raul Sanchez. Shell whistled tunelessly to himself and swung back into the saddle. He'd have Sanchez's guts for garters before the day ended.

How much more clever he was than the *estupido gringo* he had robbed the night before, El Tiburon thought to himself as he watched Shelter Morgan ride out of town and disappear over a hill. He had lost face the previous day. Now he would ride in to Julian and regain it before heading to Tecate. Oh, how Ramirez the bartender at the Cantina Sofia would roar with laughter when he heard how El Tiburon's cleverness avenged him on the *gringo*. He would, of course, not reveal all to Ramirez. Only the part that started in the saloon. He looked over at Esteban, his sole companion and nodded. Together they rode into the small mining town.

"*Hola!* I am back," he called out as he rode down the main street. "See? El Tiburon has triumphed again. I showed that one, did I not?" In front of the saloon, he and Esteban halted and tied their horses to a hitchrail. Their boots clumped loudly on the boardwalk.

Inside, Sanchez repeated his brags, adding that anyone was a sucker when they dealt rawly with El Tiburon. He strode boldly to the bar and slapped down some of Morgan's money.

"Bring me tequila and that woman the *gringo* had last night. I am going to fuck her until her eyes cross. Show her what a *real* man is like."

"I think she's done found that out," the apron snapped back. "She's sure enough wore out this morning."

"Not like she will be when I get through with her. *Andele.* Be

66

quick about it."

Lavinia's sleepy features rearranged into loathing when she saw Raul Sanchez standing at the bar, eyeing her lustfully and rubbing his crotch. She stopped on the bottom step and would come no further.

"I have it!" Sanchez burbled. "I will take her right here. In front of everyone. Let them see how *macho* El Tiburon really is."

"Oh, no you won't," the barman growled. "You'll not be having any sort of orgy in my place. Take her upstairs or in the back room, or I'll send her back to bed."

Sanchez started to protest, then saw the twin black holes of a sawed-off shotgun resting on the bar, only inches from his protruding belly. "Have it your way, then. El Tiburon feels generous today. All I know is that I must fuck that one so that my revenge is complete on the *gringo*." He shrugged and crossed to Lavinia.

"Come along, my lovely little *puta*. We will be magnificent together. With every stroke I shall think of this Morgan. Kill my men, will he? Humiliate me beyond endurance, eh? Such foolish nerve. No man stands against El Tiburon and wins!"

Shelter Morgan sat his mount easily in the thicket of pines on the edge of Julian. He had easily followed Raul Sanchez's tracks, noted where he met up with the other bandit, the one that had fled from his guns the day before. Shell continued to track them easily until they swung off the road and headed into the brushy country. A short time later he came upon his belongings.

They had not been well hidden and certainly not a permanent cache. A grim smile creased the seams around Morgan's full lips. He had a good idea what Sanchez had in mind. With most of his property back in his hands, he rode on, eyes on the faint trail that led him exactly where he expected. Now he tipped back the brim of his hat and the smile returned. With a

67

nudge of his heels, his big-chested black trotted into Julian.

His entry went nearly unnoticed. Shell stopped at the livery and left the Winchester and saddle for George Wilson. Armed with his own, he strode down the street.

"Lookie who's here?" one local drawled. "Didn't figger to see you again, mister."

"Where is Sanchez?"

His question brought surprising results. Several idlers and a dozen or so women broke out in rapturous smiles and pointed to the saloon. Shelter nodded his thanks and stepped off in that direction.

". . . *Que linda es Jalisco? Palabra no llore.*" Raul Sanchez crooned in a cracked voice as he embraced Lavinia again. This time he crouched on the bed behind her. His arms encircled her waist and he thrust forward between her open legs until he felt the hot moistness of her abused mound and plunged his raging tip into its silken confines.

"This time I won't go off so fast, that I promise you," he told the soiled dove. "But then, what does it matter. You get paid for every time."

"At the rate you've been going, I'll be a millionaire by the end of the day," Lavinia retorted.

Raul paused in mid-stroke. "How is that?"

"What you lack in size, you sure make up for in speed," Lavinia jeered.

"You are unkind, woman. You must be nice to El Tiburon, or bad things will happen."

"Not to me they won't." Lavinia had made her self feel nothing, blotted out all sensation, even when once the rutting Mexican had nearly driven her to a peak of ecstacy. What he would get would not be what he sought.

"Would you like a taste of my whip? Some women do, you know."

Before Lavinia could answer, the door burst open.

Raul's head snapped around and he looked into the muzzle a Winchester, held purposefully in the hands of his latest robbery victim. His mouth gaped and he could not take his eyes from the small black hole. He tried a smile, which turned into a twitching grimace.

"*Amigo!*" he cried in feigned delight. "So nice to see you again."

"Make a move and I'll gladly blow your brains all over the ceiling," Shell growled as he stepped forward and shoved the open end of the rifle under Raul's nostrils.

"Am I glad to see you, Shell," Lavinia began as she eased her body out from under Sanchez's bulk. In the free air, the bandit's organ instantly went slack. "Thanks for coming by. I was afraid I would die of boredom any minute now."

"Put something on, Lavinia, I think you'll want to watch what I have in mind." Shell instructed. He looked at Raul's nakedness and smiled bleakly. "You're properly dressed for the party I have in mind, El Tiburon. Ease yourself off that bed and we'll get on with it."

Had he forgotten some holiday? Tom Plaskoe wondered about that as he rode into town on the wagon seat. It appeared that the entire populace of Julian had turned out for some special event. Shouts raised and peals of laughter. Then he saw the reason.

Even without clothes, Plaskoe easily recognized the rutting little bantam who called himself El Tiburon. He stood in the center of the street, a block from the end of town, clad only in boots and sombrero. A tough-looking feller prodded him with a Winchester and trailed the local gentry and a flock of shrill-voiced little boys. The parade stopped a hundred yards short of the ore wagon. The tall stranger began to lecture Sanchez.

"I hope you have discovered the same thing I have," the bronze-tanned man began. "Stealing from people seems to be a

69

losing proposition. First you lost your guns and two of you
men, now you have lost all your clothes and, as an adde
inducement for you to mend the errors of your ways, you
horse. I'm interested, *amigo*, in what you think of all this?"

"*Companiero!*" Raul wailed. "Surely you can see that it is a
a mistake. How could anyone think I would rob my good frien'
Shel-tor. Did you find me with any of your possessions, an
other stolen goods? *¡Absolutamente no!* They have bee
recovered as I can see. Obviously they were elsewhere than o
my person. Can I be held responsible for the misdeeds o
others? Certainly it must be in your heart to see that I spea
the truth? We are partners, *amigos*, bold and resourcefu
bandidos who will become legend in both Californias."

The sharp report of the Winchester cut off his protests
Astounded, deeply in shock, Sanchez looked down to see hi
body whole and unscarred. The slug had plowed a trough in th
decomposed granite of the roadway between his legs. *Madre d
Dios*, he thought wildly. An inch or two higher and his lovelif
would never have been the same.

"Time for us to bid a fond farewell to each other," a grin
baritone voice rumbled from the man with the Winchester.

"B-but," Raul stammered amid the laughter and jeers of th
village boys and men, "you can't send me out there wit
nothing but boots and a sombrero. How ever can I survive?"

"I have this horrible suspicion that you will do just fine. I'
shoot you down like a dog," the voice went on inexorably an
Raul shuddered in recollection of the position of love in whic
he had been surprised. "But you don't have a weapon of you
own. Now get out of here or I'll reconsider and plunk a hole i
your fat carcass anyway."

With an angry shout, Raul's henchman burst through th
crowd, wildly waving a rusty Colt. His eyes glowed with
certain madness and he yelled defiance at any who would s
degrade and humiliate the great El Tiburon. The whole per
formance would have been ludicrous, had he not gripped th
.36 Navy revolver with determination, the gray spheres of th

70

ead balls visible in each chamber. Neither Raul nor Tom Plaskoe saw the Winchester move off its original target.

Faster than any could follow, Shelter Morgan swung the rifle toward the young bandit and triggered off another round. Youth and hot blood kept the wiry Mexican on his feet, though he staggered back a step. His face contorted in rage and hurt and he took slow, deliberate aim.

The hammer fell on a percussion cap. Only a small *pfutt* sounded a split-second before Shelter's Winchester blasted a third time. Cloth flew from the youthful bandit's shirt and his hand went slack. The Colt thudded in the gravel of the street a moment before his knees sagged and he gave up his spirit with a soft sigh and toppled face-first in the dirt.

Instantly Shell whipped back around to Raul. "You have any great urge to be next?"

"No. Oh, no, *amigo*. He was a bad one, that Esteban. I . . . I think I will leave now. *Adios, Señor*."

With the speed of the gunshots, Tom Plaskoe recognized the man with the Winchester. Captain Shelter Morgan. But that couldn't be, his mind clamored. Morgan had died in Georgia on a cold, foggy day. How could he be here now? A chill ran down Plaskoe's spine. That feeling of being watched, hunted by someone. Was Shelter Morgan real, alive? Or . . . or was he a ghost, come to haunt all those who had been a part of that ancient betrayal? Either way, he did not want to stay around to find out. Slowly he climbed from the wagon seat, hopeful his movement would not attract Morgan's attention.

"Sammy, take the gold to the freight station and unload. Be sure to get a receipt for it. Then go get the provisions and head back to the mine."

"Sure thing, Mister Plaskoe." Sammy's adenoidal voice hid his disappointment.

"And, Sammy . . . ah, don't get any notions about that Gatling gun. Leave it where it is. If anyone asks about me, tell 'em I was too busy to come in person. Mine business, you understand?"

71

"Anything you say, Mister Plaskoe."

Tom took his horse from the back of the wagon. He tightened the cinch and swung into the saddle. He drummed his heels into the beast's flanks and cantered out of town in the direction from which they had come.

"I'd be obliged to buy you a drink," the old prospector from whom Shelter had borrowed the rifle and saddle told him once the crowd broke up and went its way behind the undertaker's wagon.

"I could use one," Morgan admitted. They walked along amicably until they reached the entrance of the first saloon.

Inside Shelter was greeted with shouts of approval and congratulations.

"We'll not be seein' ol' Tiburon's face around here for a long while," one man speculated.

"You can count on that," George Wilson agreed. "Sanchez was braggin' up something about you bein' a friend of Tom Plaskoe's. That right?"

The comment raised Morgan's eyebrows. "In a manner of speaking. We served together in the War."

"Well, his wagon's in town. Normally he comes along. Nobody but that dimwitted kid, Sammy Grimes, came today. Matter of fact, this is the first time I recollect Plaskoe not bein' along. He watches that gold like a hawk. If you came here figgerin' to see him, might be you can ride along with the kid when he goes back."

"Good idea. I'll look into that." Morgan finished his drink, refused half a dozen warm-hearted offers for more and strolled out on the main street. Down the way he saw an ore wagon and headed for it.

Although considered a dolt by the people of Julian, Sammy Grimes could not be called mentally deficient. He had simply chosen to be stupid. His needs in life were simple. His pimply face, a legacy since his eleventh year, had kept him at some

72

distance from girls his own age. That he didn't mind too much. By the time the heat of sexual arousal burned in his loins he had come to learn he could always lope his mule for relief or go to that sissy Godfrey boy to have it licked and slurped on. Then he had learned about ladies of the evening.

This great revelation eventually caused him, at the tender age of sixteen, to take the owlhoot trail. So obsessed had he become with wetting his wick in those warm and slippery bodies that he had been compelled to steal so he could obtain funds to support his habit. The town constable nearly caught him rifling the general mercantile one night and he had to flee the small town in Arizona Territory where he had been born and grown up. The year since had not lessened his drive, only decreased the frequency with which he could indulge it. All the way to Julian his mind had been filled with lurid visions of a certain willing young miss who lived on the edge of town. Already notorious, though three years younger than he, she entertained all comers who could get it up, young, old or in between.

His boss's orders to load up and return at once got in the way of this dreamed-of indulgence. It didn't serve to slacken the rigidity of his pecker, though, and he found himself distracted as to what to do first. Should he unload the gold or get the supplies? Devoid of logic, Sammy finally figured out that he couldn't put one thing in until he took the other out. He settled for the freight office. If he hurried, he reasoned dimly, he might even have time to put something else in a softer, juicier place. So absorbed had he become in the image of that chubby, nearly hairless mound that he jumped when the man whom he had seen run the bandido out of town came up and spoke to him.

"Huh?" Sammy gasped.

"I asked if you happened to be Sammy Grimes?"

"Yup. That's me, mister. Who wants to know?"

"I'm a friend of your boss. Ol' Tom and I go back to the War. We fought in the same outfit."

"Well, that's mighty nice, I'm sure. What's that got to do with me?"

"I hear Tom didn't come in this time."

"He did and he didn't," Sammy evaded, unsure of this smooth-talking man. "That is, he rode to the edge of town with me. Then he all of a sudden swung up on his hoss and rode off back to the mine. That was just after we saw you give a shelackin' to them two Mezkins."

"It must have been something important," Shelter speculated aloud. Inwardly, he figured that his quarry had no doubt recognized him and made hurried tracks to put some distance between them. "I'm sure sorry to miss ol' Tom. Came all the way up here to visit, too. Say . . ." the vengeance-minded Morgan added as though the idea had only occurred to him. "I wonder, would it be all right if I were to ride out to the mine with you?"

There goes my chance to see Sally, Sammy thought dismally. Then a flash of inspiration came to him. Why not use this stranger's comin' along to account for a little delay? A slow smile formed on Sammy's thin lips.

"I don't see why not. Sure, mister. You bein' a friend and all, there can't be anything wrong with that. I'll be ready in, ah, say two, maybe three hours. I'll meet you back here at the shipping office."

"Done, then."

9.

Reflected moonlight rippled across the gently undulating wavelets of a small land-locked cove on the southern tip of Bahia de Los Angeles half way down the peninsula of Baja California, on the Sea of Cortez. The slatted streak of brightness looked like some sort of fairy ladder that would let the observer climb it to the craggy surface of the moon itself. On a sandy shelf of this protected shore, palm-frond shelters, called *palapas*, had been erected to provide for the comfort of El Guillo's men, their permanent women and some two dozen scrawny, naked children.

When the bandit gang first arrived, they set the women to making repairs on the roofs of the open-sided palapas, while they built huge fire pits to roast halves of beef and whole pigs and goats. The men also commenced to consume prodigious quantities of tequila and beer. The new women were used as slaves, all except Maria Elena.

She had withdrawn with El Guillo himself and, when the camp began to settle down after dark, her quick mind brought to her a possible chance for escape and rescue. The cliff behind the beach was steep and sheer, though not too much so to prevent climbing. She knew she could do it. First, though, she had to put El Guillo to sleep. Coyly, she reached for his fly and opened his trousers while his dark-shadowed jaws ground away on juicy goatmeat cooked to a crispy outside and contained in a fresh-made corn tortilla.

"Hummm. You are a good girl, like the *gringo* said. You know what a man needs after a hard day's work."

Maria Elena extracted his semi-rigid member from his trousers and bent forward. Slowly she rubbed the silky tip against her cheek. It brought more murmurs of pleasure from her captor. In her mind she girded herself for what she must do.

Several years ago, before her fourteenth year, she was certain, she and a close friend had used this method, taking turns, to exhaust a particularly vigorous young caballero from a rancho outside her town. He bragged that no girl could satisfy him in a single night and that he had worn out most who tried. His arrogant boasts irritated the girls in the village, few of whom he had actually had opportunity to experiment with. Together, the girls hatched their plan.

That time it had been he, who weak and shaken, could barely crawl from the small shed behind Maria's house and pull himself up into the saddle, long before sunrise, for the ride to the rancho. The girls had giggled and hugged each other in their triumph. Their own needs had not been satisfied, for they had not used those slippery openings between their legs. They made do with the poor substitute of each other's eager fingers that night. The next day they found a willing, but slightly confused boy of their own age to give them what they most loved. Now, Maria Elena proposed to perform the ordeal alone.

Her facile tongue replaced her cheek and began to inscribe lazy spirals around the fat tip of El Guillo's rigid, pulsing organ. He groaned in delight.

She worked on, rolling and caressing the staff to its base, then back up again. Then she plunged it deep into her mouth, lips nuzzling and teasing, tongue licking frantically. El Guillo writhed.

When at last he reached his peak and a million sensations set his body to trembling and cramping, she did not release him for even a second of calm. On she worked, and on. Incapable of coherent speech and stimulated beyond any past experience, he thrashed in the chair. El Guillo squealed.

By the time he had expelled his sap a second time he had

begun to weaken slightly. Still she showed him no mercy. Too much pleasure can become painful and El Guillo neared the point of such an experience as she continued to tug and pull on his manhood with tightly gripping lips that seemed determined to uproot his staff and swallow it whole. El Guillo bellowed.

Maria Elena never relented. If anything, her strength seemed to increase. Powerfully, hungrily, she worked toward a third eruption, dragging along tingling reverberations from the last. It took a long while. El Guillo howled.

After the fourth cataclysm, which had taken a great deal of time to achieve, Maria Elena's jaws began to ache so severely she feared a cramp, yet she gave no quarter. Beyond the ability to do anything but *feel*, El Guillo did not protest. El Guillo moaned.

Not another soul stirred in the camp and El Guillo lay like one entranced, eyes slitted and glassy, no longer conscious of anything or sensation beyond the ending tugging at his aching organ, a painful experience now, which he was powerless to end because of the unending pleasure it brought. The sixth thrilling ascent to the pinnacle began deep in his belly. El Guillo whined weakly.

Not a sound came from El Guillo, save gentle snoring, when Maria Elena took his limp sausage from her mouth and rose from her position between his legs. His last two crescendoes, the ninth and tenth, had been dry, lacking even a hint of the precious sap that he had valiantly discharged through the long, endless evening. For a short while, between them, El Guillo had sobbed.

For a moment, Maria feared her jaw would never work again. She massaged the aching muscles with one hand while she sought about the darkness under the palapa for a few items she would need.

She located a large canteen and a small revolver, wrapped a thick slab of goat meat in a cheesecloth, along with tortillas and chopped onions, and a hat to cover her head. Another quick check of El Guillo and she slipped off into the night.

Climbing the cliff proved harder than she had anticipated. It took her well into the early hours of morning before the pale light of the sky could be seen above the darker line of the top. She made it at last and scrabbled down the more gentle back side. A long way still separated her from her goal, though she set off with a light heart across what would become a scorching desert with the rising sun. Safety lay ahead.

Soon, she kept telling herself, she would be safe at the church in El Crucero.

Tom Plaskoe had ridden all night. The spectre of Shelter Morgan drove him to recklessness. He reached the mine a short while after sunrise. Half a day, the fastest he had ever covered the distance. Quickly he called to his men.

"Mike, Dave. Get out here. We've got trouble."

"What is it, Boss?" Mike Struthers rumbled as he came from the small shelter shrugging into a shirt.

"Remember I was jumpy the other night? It wasn't my imagination, boys. There's a man hunting for me. He's in Julian, but that don't say he wasn't here watching earlier. He'll probably follow the wagon right back here. We've got to set up an ambush so we can hit him before he gets close to the mine."

"What's he after you for?"

"It's an old story, Dave. One I don't have time to go into now. Trust me. He's only one man. We can kill him and none will be the wiser."

"He a lawman?" Mike wanted to know.

"No."

"Bounty hunter?"

"No, Dave. Though he could be, there's no wanted flyer on me."

"Who is he, then?"

"His name's Shelter Morgan. He was a captain in the Army of Tennessee."

"Hell, you Rebs lost the war. He can't be huntin' you as

78

a deserter."

Time nibbled at Plaskoe's mind like a starving rat at a child's toes. He wanted to be moving, doing something to lay a surprise for Shelter Morgan. "I didn't desert . . . not in so many words. Though, in one way, I suppose I did. Me'n some forty other guys . . . along with some gold this Captain Morgan had taken a big chance to bring down outta Tennessee, right under the noses of the Yankees."

"An' you stold it?" Mike asked in awe.

"Uh . . . sort of. That's . . . that's what I first used as gold comin' out of this mine."

"Well, I'll be damned. Dave, we'n the Boss had best get goin'. Wouldn't be right not to welcome this here gold hunter, now would it?"

Meadowlarks and orioles had taken a mid-morning siesta and the vast valleys amid the peaks of the Cuyamachas lay in silence, except for the clop of the mule's hoofs and Shelter's big black. He rode beside the ore wagon, glancing occasionally at the pimply youth who sat on the spring-mounted seat.

"You work for Tom long?"

"'Bout a year now," came Sammy's sparse reply.

"I hear he has struck it rich."

"Oh, he has that. In a way lots of folks wouldn't expect, either. That's his secret."

"How's that?"

"Cain't tell you. He'd have my hide off me if I did. Reckon if he wants you to know, he'll fill you in hisself." He breathed deeply. His loins still vibrated from the powerful good fuckin' he'd had with Sally. She really knew how to throw it around. They'd gone after it three times. The first hadn't been much. He'd shot his load when Sally gave him a good hard bump with her muff after only two nice long strokes. It had been too long, she told him and right away got him worked up to try again. He took a deep breath now and the world felt good.

"Mighty nice air up here," he volunteered. "Ain't like Arizona."

"That where you hail from?"

Suspicion clouded Sammy's eyes. "You by any chance from there? A lawman or something?"

"No. I come from Tennessee."

"Tennessee, huh? Where's that?"

Shelter hid his grin. "A long ways from here. In the South."

"Oh. That's right, you said you'd been in the war with Mister Plaskoe."

"Un-huh," Morgan acknowledged dryly. "Thought I'd drop by and recall old times with him."

Mike and Dave Dring waited on one side of the trail, Tom Plaskoe on the other. They had a perfect place, where the narrow road turned a bend and entered a cluster of live oaks that screened passers-by from the jumble of boulders and anything else on the sides of the path. Near mid-afternoon, the rattle of the big ore wagon could be clearly heard. Where would Morgan be? Plaskoe thought on it as he watched Sammy come into view and draw near.

Damn! There was Morgan riding right beside the kid. Stupid thing to do. But he didn't know which one had been stupid. Chances were it would be Sammy. Plaskoe brought up his Spencer and fitted it to his shoulder.

Across the way, a frown creased Mike's forehead. "Take it easy," he cautioned Dave in a whisper. "We don't want to hit the kid."

Dave nodded and eased his rifle from the notch in his shoulder.

Plaskoe fired. The bullet went wide, striking a boulder a few yards behind Shelter Morgan and screaming off through the mountain air. Startled, Sammy whipped the mules into a gallop and bounded down the trail with the lightly loaded wagon. Morgan jumped his horse forward and crowded up into the rocks on the same side as Plaskoe.

His mind worked rapidly. Given the ambush, Plaskoe must have recognized him in Julian, the manhunter realized. He dismounted and moved cautiously through the boulders. Plaskoe got a glimpse of him and fired again.

Another miss.

Suddenly shots opened up on him from two places across the trail. Under the diversion, Plaskoe rushed from his hiding place and flagged Sammy down to a slow roll. He swung aboard the wagon on the off-side from where Morgan waited with his Winchester ready.

"Get going. Back to the mine. Let the others handle Morgan."

"But he . . . he said he was a friend of yours," Sammy protested.

"He lied. He's here to kill me. I know it." More miserably he thought of how this particular means of disposing of the stolen gold had come to an end. People will wonder what happened to the stranger who had identified himself as a friend of his. There was already a lot of talk about how lucky he had been. It wouldn't be long before the Dorado Mine would be exposed as the front it was. By that time, he wanted to be long gone.

Bullets cut through the branches of crinkly, dark green oak leaves and sent showers of the spike-edged bits raining down on Shelter Morgan. He spotted his enemies and took careful aim.

A slug screamed off rock in front of Dave's head. He yelped and ducked low. Instantly, Shelter Morgan rushed from his former spot, headed for the high ground where he could get a view down on his attackers.

The two gunmen turned out to be better than he had expected. He no sooner reached his chosen spot than shots filled the space between them and slugs howled among the rocks at his back. They, too, had changed position. Quickly Shell blasted off a reply and ran again.

Plaskoe's henchmen seemed to be everywhere. They worked their way around the sloping hillside and took more shots at the man ducking low in the boulders. Shelter Morgan, Plaskoe had named him. He knew his business, Harry allowed. Slowly, the senior gunslinger observed, they were driving this Morgan further from his horse and higher up the opposite hill.

"Next time he shoots and runs, we cross over, Dave," he told his partner.

"Gotcha."

Three fast rounds from Morgan's Winchester sent both men sprawling. As the reports echoed off, Harry came to his feet.

"Now!"

A plan had begun to form in Shelter's head. Above him to the right he saw a dark spot, no doubt the entrance to some played-out or abandoned mine. He got off a quick round that smashed the heel from the younger ambusher's boot and used the moment of confusion to race upslope to the promising place of refuge.

He had been right, Shell saw when he dived for cover into the opening in the hill. Sagging timbers shored up an old mine. He settled himself and peered downward in search of his targets.

They showed themselves, rushing across a narrow open strip. Shell already had his Winchester to his shoulder when he heard a rustling sound behind him. Following it came a hiss and a burring rattle. He swung and fired instinctively.

His first slug slammed into the thick bulk of a huge rattler, fully six or more feet long. Vicious even in death, the wounded reptile forced itself forward, again coiling to strike. This time Morgan put the bullet into its head, smashing the large triangle into pulp.

The headless snake went wild, heaving and thrashing on the floor of the mine tunnel, deprived of sight, smell and mind. After a shuddery moment, Shell ignored it and turned his attention back to the major threat outside.

"Hear them shots?" Dave asked Mike.

"Yeah. He's in that old mine. We got him trapped now."

"You men out there. Do you work for Tom Plaskoe?"

"Uh . . . that's right," Mike called back at the disembodied voice coming from the mine. "He said you was out to kill him."

"I am. What do you know of his gold and where it came from?"

"Work your way around that way, Dave," Mike whispered. "I'll keep him wrapped up talkin' until you get into place to blast him." After Dave slipped off through the brush and boulders, Mike called out to Morgan.

"We know now it was stolen. You're name's Morgan, right? Shelter Morgan?"

"That's me. Tell me all you know about Plaskoe."

"He come to California shortly after the war. I guess he had all that gold and wanted some way to dispose of it. Anyhow he bought this mine, the Dorado. Started smeltin' down the good gold and recasting ingots. Make a long story short, about four years ago he ran out. That's when we came into the game. Also this Mezkin bandit, El Guillo."

"Tell me about him. I've heard the name recently."

"El Guillo operates in Baja California. Robs other Mezkins. He an' Paskoe have a deal goin'. Paskoe helps El Guillo scoop up valuables in Baja and converts them into hard cash."

"I thought there was little love lost between the Mexicans and us. Why would this El Guillo let a *gringo* sign up with his bandits?"

Mike laughed. "That's the best part. Ya see, some time back, before he used up all his own gold, Plaskoe ran into this Master Sergeant who had deserted from the Army over in Arizona. Well, he had along a couple of wagons an' you know what was in them?"

"No. But tell me. I'm curious."

You won't be much longer, Mike thought as he watched Dave maneuver for a spot where he could see into the cave without being spotted himself. "Why, he had a Gatling gun and enough ammo to keep it firin' until Gabriel blows the last call. Plaskoe bought it an' that gave him a trump card with them Mexes. They can forget a lot of things when it comes to crackin' open banks and such like with the ease that Gatling does it. He brought us in on the deal and we've been doing nicely ever since."

"Where does Plaskoe keep the Gatling gun?"

"Takes it wherever he goes. It was in that wagon you rode in with. Surprised he would have left it with Sammy. The kid ain't too bright." Mike looked up and saw Dave in position. An evil smile illuminated his face, only to fade when Dave rose and walked forward, giving his head a puzzled shake.

Dave neared the tunnel and moved cautiously to one side. He waited a long moment, then inched forward, his Colt barrel leading the way. A moment later he entered and disappeared from Mike's view.

To his amazement, Dave found the low tunnel empty except for a headless rattlesnake that continued to writhe on the floor as though possessed of life. A moment later he heard a metallic clatter and glanced up to come face to face with Shelter Morgan.

"Oh . . . shit!" Dave managed before Shelter's Winchester exploded in his face.

Below the entrance, Mike heard the shot and breathed easier. "You get him, Dave?"

"Yep," Morgan answered back for the dead man at his feet.

Filled with confidence and relief now, Mike ambled up the hill. He reached the tailings of the old mine and skirted them, to come out on a small level stretch, the last place he had seen Dave. In the next instant, a stranger stepped out of the tunnel.

With barely three feet separating them, Morgan fired into Mike's belly.

The outlaw bent double and fell into a writhing heap. Another bullet to his head ended the misery and splashed around human brains with the same ease a previous one had cleaned out a rattlesnake skull.

Two of them down, Morgan thought with satisfaction. "Now for Plaskoe," he spoke aloud.

10.

According to the kid, Sammy, only three of them worked for Plaskoe. That meant only two more to face, Shelter Morgan thought as he made his way up toward the mine. He reloaded his Winchester and loosened the Colt in its holster. Innate caution, and the combat skills born of the long, sad conflict between the States, sent him in a wide circle, so that he could approach at an unexpected angle. A huge oak on the edge of the clearing gave him his final observation point. So far he had seen no sign of life around the dark hole of the mine entrance or the small adobe and wood structure off to one side. Morgan waited there a long ten minutes to satisfy himself that another ambush had not been set up for him. Then, keeping low to the ground, he made a dash for the low roofed building set between two only slightly smaller oaks.

Shelter's Winchester led the way into the two-room bunkhouse. He found no one. Spilled drawers and overturned items of furniture indicated a hasty rifling and departure. Moving silently, he quickly searched both rooms, then stepped back out into the waning afternoon sunshine. That left the mine.

The oar wagon sat to the right of the tunnel, back to the rock face, tailgate removed. Something was being loaded, an obvious conclusion Morgan realized as he advanced on the scene. He still saw no sign of anyone. At the timber-shored entrance he paused to listen.

At first he heard nothing, neither the breathing of a person waiting for him in the dark, nor any sounds of feverish activity. Then, dimly, as from a great distance, he made out a metallic clank and scraping noises. Reassured, Morgan entered the mine.

In a nitch carved into the wall a few feet from the opening, he located three carbide miner's lamps. He opened one and charged it with union carbide from a barrel so marked, adding water from a canteen that dangled from a spike in the shoring. He quickly screwed the top on and opened the valve, then spun the flint wheel and sparked it to life. He adjusted the band to fit around his hat and put the hands-off light into place. Guided by its sere white beams, he advanced.

A hundred yards into the granite hillside, a gentle slope angled downward to the second drift level. At the bottom of that incline, Sammy Grimes labored to drag a heavy piece of a metal smelter into position to be winched upward by a cable suspended from a drum on a crossbar above. When Shell's light rays fell on the young outlaw, he jerked as though slapped.

"Harry? Is that you, Harry? Dave?" He shielded his eyes with one hand in an attempt to see beyond the glare.

"No, Sammy. It's Shelter Morgan."

Sammy stood erect, one hand resting on the butt of his .36 Navy. "How did you get here?"

"Harry and Dave are dead, Sammy. I didn't want to kill them, but they got in the way. Where's Tom Plaskoe? He's the one I'm after."

"He ain't here, Mister Morgan."

"Where is he, Sammy? Tell me about it."

"He took off. We loaded the Gatling gun on that cart of his and he headed south like a fury. Left me here to load the smelter and come after him. He's gone to Mexico, to Baja California."

"I ought to take you in to the law in Julian, Sammy. I could, but I want Tom Plaskoe. So I'll give you a break. You can go your way and I'll go mine."

For an instant, Sammy looked sad. "Can't do that, Mister Morgan."

"Of course you can, Sammy."

"Mister Plaskoe left me to do a job. He's relyin' on me. I . . . I guess I'll have to shoot you."

"No! I don't want to kill you, Sammy, but I will. Put down that gun, come up here and head out on your own."

"Mister Plaskoe's the only one ever treated me like a man. I . . . I *owe* it to him!"

Sammy yanked the Colt free from leather and, like the amateur he was, jerked the trigger before the gun locked into position. The lens of the carbide lamp intercepted the ball an instant before it punched through the crown of Shelter's Stetson, whipping the hat from his head. It snapped Shelter's head back a moment and caused his own shot to go wild. The only light now came from Sammy's miner's lamp. Shell quickly levered another round into the chamber as Sammy eared back the hammer cap-and-ball pistol.

Morgan fired first. His bullet struck Sammy square in the chest. Its impact at such short range drove the boy back over the input hopper he had dragged into place under the winch. His legs kicked feebly for a few seconds, then went still. During that short while, Shelter Morgan felt deep, genuine regret. During his long quest he had killed a lot of men. Men who deserved it. Had any of them possessed only a little of Sammy's kind of blind loyalty for the Cause of the South, they would never have committed murder and stolen the gold. And . . . they would have never become targets for Shelter Morgan. Slowly he turned and made his way out of the mine.

Plaskoe had a good head start, traveling in a light cart which would give him almost as much ground covering ability as a man on horseback. He also had the advantage of knowing where he was going. He would have to meet up with El Guillo, that Morgan took for granted. Only where?

El Guillo paced the strand in a fury. Two nights ago, Maria Elena had escaped. How had she managed that? No trails led into the cove, which seemed scooped out of the high granite cliff walls by a huge hand. No boats had been stolen. Only one small craft remained anyway, in which he had sent his trusted lieutenant, Juan Rubio, to summon the bargeman so that they could get on the move. No telling about the girl. She might go to the Rurales and then again, she might not. People of her class rarely wanted anything to do with the law. One thing he knew for certain.

He could wait no longer. He and his men must head for the rendezvous with the *gringo*. He kicked at a clump of sea grass, washed ashore by a storm the night before. Naked children squealed and splashed in the water nearby. They would be unhappy returning to their usual life so soon. It was necessary, though. Within a week's time his gang had to be in position to take their next target, El Crucero.

Plaskoe had to hurry! He had only six days left in which to reach a spot a day's ride from El Crucero. Driven not only by the vision of a vengeful Shelter Morgan, but also by the need to meet and plan a new means of converting their loot into useful and untraceable ingots, Tom Plaskoe punished his draft animal into sweat-foaming exertion. He had taken a different trail than his usual, one that forked a few miles from the border.

On the western branch now, rather than the one that led to the desert, he headed toward Tecate and the legendary trail down the spine of Baja, the Route of the Padres. Already most of the missions, convents and schools established along this eighteenth century trail had fallen to disuse and decay.

A few towns had sprung up around these old churches. Towns that would eventually be raided by El Guillo. Meanwhile, they also meant the only chance for survival in the hostile, desert-like mountains of Baja for the fleeing man. It would, he thought, give him a chance to study them for their future fate. Although provided with this means of hope,

Plaskoe's mind still went back to Shelter Morgan and the fight at the mine.

Harry and Dave would be able to stop the former captain. They had to be. Yet, if they didn't, that would mean Morgan would come on after him. Relentless, deliberate. How had Morgan learned that he had gone to California? Or about the mine? Questions drove at him as he lashed the reins on his fleet-footed mule's rump.

Shelter Morgan returned to the living quarters. Perhaps he could find something that would indicate where Plaskoe might be going to meet with El Guillo. He made a more meticulous search this time. Among the items he found was a crudely executed map of Baja California. He spread it on the table and bent to examine it closely.

A pencil line had been drawn beside the dotted symbol for a trail. It led to the east, down the mountain slopes in Mexico and out onto the desert. There it turned south and proceeded to a point where it rose again into the southern Lagunas, called the Sierra San Pedro Martir by the Mexicans. Notations, in a small, crabbed hand, appeared at intervals along the route. Shell read them aloud.

"'No water here. Three tall spires on your left. Soft sand. Look for twin peaks to the west. Sea gulls found here in winter. Turn west, last chance for pass.'" A large "X" marked a small valley in the Sierra. "'Meet Rudy here,'" the entry beside it read.

One question still remained for Shelter to ponder. Did Plaskoe always meet the bandits at that spot?

Another pencil mark traced a line along the center of the Baja peninsula, following a roadway that the legend said was no longer through. The stroke ended near a small village named El Crucero. One or the other, this time? He had to make a choice. Shell folded the map and placed it in the pocket of his shirt. Then he headed for the door.

And nearly bowled over Raul Sanchez.

A broad, triumphant smile spread on the bandit's face. Fully clothed now, with a more modern choice of weapons, he stood eyeing Shelter Morgan with a cold and baleful stare. His thumb wrapped around the hammer of a Smith and Wesson .44 American and drew it back.

"El barco viene!" a lookout called an hour before sundown. The shout lightened El Guillo's day. Relieved, his thoughts turned to the future.

They would make one, perhaps two more big, sweeping raids. Then there would be money enough. He could leave this life, purchase a big estancia and settle down to the role of *Patron* to the people who worked his land. Perhaps in Sonora, or near Guaymas, so his son could enjoy the sea. Maybe even on the high, mountainous plateau near Carretero, birthplace of Mexico's independence from Spain. He would like that. First there was work to do.

"Pablo, Marco, Xavier, hurry. Get the men to loading their bundles down on the beach. You women," he yelled to those still packing or tending cook fires. "Put out the fires, gather your children and take those packages to the beach. Hurry."

El Guillo stooped to swing one small, naked boy, who had been swimming and splashing at the water's edge, high into the air, then hugged him to his bare chest. The dripping youngster shrilled and wriggled. He ruffled the squealing child's thick mop of black hair and kissed the boy. He had reached seven years. That much Rudolfo Santacruz knew because little Pepito was his son. He had been born only a few months before death had taken his mother, the only woman El Guillo had ever truly loved. The loss had saddened him. Yet, he had his son and wished to leave a better legacy for the youngster than the life of a bandido.

"You will be going back to your *Tia* Margarita," he told the lad. "I want you to be a good boy, Pepito. You are all I have."

"*Si, Papi.* My mother is in heaven, *verdad?*"

For a brief instant, tears came to El Guillo's eyes. "Yes, son. Yes, she is. May the Angels watch over her. I must go away and work again. When I next return, we shall be rich as the *hacendados* with their big ranchos."

"Really, *Papi?* Will I have a horse of my own?"

El Guillo laughed. "You will have a herd of them if you want, *niño.* Now, run along and find your clothes. You will be going back where people are."

Pepito frowned, the effort wrinkling his button nose. "I do not like to live with *Tia* Margarita. She makes me wear clothes, even when I swim, and that itches and feels tight in places all over. Shoes, too, which hurt my feet."

"But that is the way of the world, Pepito. Man must cover his body, so he must wear clothes."

"Why, *Papi?* Why do we have to cover our bodies? The wind and sun feel so good, the water of the sea, too. When we are rich, can we find a place to live where we will never have to wear clothes or shoes?"

"I don't think your mother would approve of that." Again tears wet El Guillo's close-set, beady eyes. He knuckled them away. "Besides, when you grow older, you will discover, ah, reasons for wanting to wear clothes. Go on and make ready, son. Soon we will be on the barge."

Raul Sanchez motioned Shelter back into the small building with the muzzle of his .44. "No more *Señor Buffon*," he growled. "I will not be humiliated like that. Say your prayers, *gringo.*"

"Raul . . . *Compañero*," Morgan started. "Dear friend, what a pleasure to see you again. Such a handsome set of clothes. Dare I ask where you got them? No doubt from one less deserving of them than yourself. You are in time to help me collect a lot of gold. And something more. Listen to this.

"Tom Plaskoe has been working with El Guillo for some

years now. There was still some gold here, which he loaded into a cart and raced away with. If we hurry we can catch him."

"Good. After I kill you, I will run him to ground and take the gold away."

"No," Morgan hastened to say. "I don't think that will work. You remember telling me that El Guillo is rumored to have great firepower for the size of his bandit gang? More than he should be expected to have? Well, Plaskoe is the one who has it. A Gatling gun. That's the more I wanted to tell you about. It is the biggest one made, with a bore of one-point-one inches. A monster. With that they can hold off an army. It will take skill and much cunning to seize the gun and the gold from Plaskoe and El Guillo. For that, even El Tiburon will need help. And I have a plan."

Two scraggly willows eked out a minimal existence on the banks of a small pool formed by a seep spring in the hills. A day's ride north of El Crucero, this oasis provided the only water for miles. El Guillo and his men reached it two days after they reclaimed their horses from a small, struggling fishing camp on the shores of the Sea of Cortez. Pepito Santacruz had buried his face in his father's broad middle and cried, begging not to be left behind, for his father not to leave him. Anything but another stay with *Tia* Margarita and her many "Uncles" who came to visit from the fishing camp. Sternly, his voice gruff, El Guillo had urged his son to have patience.

Patience is a virtue unknown to the unruly men attracted to the life of bandits. Two knife fights broke out and El Guillo had found it necessary to execute the winner of a backshooting incident. Only a steady flow of tequila, rich food and the services of two aging but eagerly willing *putas* kept the brigands in line. At last, a scout reported the approach of Plaskoe and his carreta.

Tom Plaskoe entered a camp filled with the rich odor of cooking tortillas and spitted meat, roasting with onions and chili peppers for the mid-day meal. He dismounted stiffly and gratefully accepted the offer of food.

"You are here."

"As I promised, Rudy. Is El Crucero ready for us?"

"Oh, yes. It is a beautiful little town, with pretty homes, a copper mine and a church bursting with gold. All ripe for our plucking."

"We have a problem."

"What is that, *gringo*?"

Hesitantly, Plaskoe explained what had happened at the mine. "I left one man to disassemble the smelter and bring it along."

"We will have to figure out another way. That is no problem," El Guillo assured him. "So long as you have that Gatling gun, everything else will work out."

"It will have to," Plaskoe replied. He stretched prodigiously. "I'm tired. It has taken me five days to get here. I need a good rest."

"Sleep well tonight. Tomorrow we will start for El Crucero."

The sage, manzanita and lupine of the mountains around the border had given away to sparse vegetation, mostly cactus. Heat and lack of water had slowed progress for Shelter Morgan and his companion, Raul Sanchez. They rode mostly in silence. El Tiburon licked his lips in anticipation. A famous Gatling gun . . . and gold, too.

He couldn't believe his good fortune. Why, all this *estupido gringo* Morgan wants is his life and Plaskoe's death. That should prove easy enough to arrange. Then, the Gatling would be in his hands. Why, that will make him, El Tiburon, Scourge of Baja California, the most powerful *bandido* in all Mexico. Greed still lighted his eyes as he gazed thoughtfully at the man riding beside him.

They had been deep into Baja California for three days now. From a peon working a field outside Tecate, they had learned that a man matching Plaskoe's description, driving a carreta, had taken the old road of the Padres, heading south down the mountainous center of the peninsula. The trail had not been easy to follow, but El Tiburon found this *gringo* to be an exceptional tracker. Soon they would catch up to El Guillo's bandits.

Then he would have both the gold and the gun. Yes, tonight would mark the end of the fourth day of the chase and already a dozen plans swam in his head on how to dispose of the *gringo*, Morgan.

The bandit gang reached a hill overlooking El Crucero half an hour before sundown the next day. They made a cold camp and slept well out of sight of the villagers. In the chill dawn, an hour before sunup, El Guillo roused his men.

"Take your magical gun down into position, *gringo*. I will see my men in place while you set up. When the sun rises, you will open fire."

"It should be easy enough."

"Well, uh, there is one complication. *Four*, actually."

"What are those?"

"Since we first looked over El Crucero, four *soldados* of the Mexican Army have been assigned to the town to guard the bank and the government's interest in the copper mine. They are well armed and know much better how to fight than these chicken-hearted peasants."

"Why were they brought in all of a sudden?"

"To protect the payroll for the mine that is in the bank."

"I see," Plaskoe replied. "When is that payday?"

"Why, today, *amigo*," El Guillo informed him with a laugh and a slap on the back. The thought of all that extra wealth made him feel expansive. Even toward the hated *gringo*.

"I'll get in range of the bank right off, then." Plaskoe summoned his gun crew and they took the big weapon down into position on a flat that commanded the entire village.

While Plaskoe made final adjustments and loaded the Gatling's hopper, El Guillo sent his men to both sides of town.

Eager for the gold, he sat his sturdy horse and waited.

Slowly a rose tint spread along the eastern horizon. Light came with it and roosters crowed in El Crucero. By the time human figures could be clearly seen, the inhabitants of the village had risen and started about their day's chores. A stream of men, with food-stuffed bolsas and miner's hats ambled through the streets toward the tall tin-covered building over the shaft head. A steam whistle blew, summoning the workers. Ricardo trained the Gatling according to Plaskoe's instructions and a faint smile brightened his face.

Plaskoe reached out and turned the crank.

Bedlam exploded over El Crucero.

A stream of big one inch slugs began to trash the fronts of buildings on the main street. Two soldiers rushed from the door of the bank, rifles in hands, fingers fumbling with buttons and belt harness. Plaskoe shouted for the gun to be retrained on them and spun the crank.

Both soldiers flew from their feet in a welter of gore. Blood splashed the building fronts, along with bits of uniform and chunks of flesh. The few glass pane windows along the block of commercial establishments dissolved into showers of fine shards. Women screamed and children wailed. All rushed toward the church as the men of town became aware of the cataclysm that had descended on them and ran for their weapons.

11.

The rattling fire of the Gatling gun continued to tear up and down the walls of the town's main street. Plaskoe paused frequently to allow the barrels to be swabbed and more ammunition to be added to the hopper. Two more soldiers ran into the street.

"There. Train on them soldier-boys," Plaskoe shouted.

Both men knelt and took steady aim. A slug cracked past Plaskoe's head, close enough to be heard over the roar of the Gatling. Then his trainer depressed the gun enough and a pair of fat one inch bullets literally tore the soldier in two as they pulped flesh and separated his spine an inch below his chest. The other uniformed man, a corporal, fired again.

Ricardo cried out and slumped away from the gun, a wide red stain spreading on his left shoulder.

"Manuel, up here!" Plaskoe cried. Manuel leaped into the carreta.

Quickly the huge Gatling came into play again. A line of dust plumes ran over the soldier who resisted. He threw his arms wide and flopped backward, his chest a ruin.

"Get your arms! Stand and fight. Hurry men of El Crucero!"

Among the buildings of the town, Padre Miguel Espinosa shouted to the villagers, rallying the men, directing women and children to the church. When he saw the soldier die, he thought momentarily of rushing forward and grabbing up the thrown rifle. But, no, he was a man of God, a man of peace.

"Hurry. Get someone onto the roofs. Three men can't be all.

96

This is the gang of El Guillo," Padre Miguel shouted. A lock of black, curly hair fell across his high forehead. His handsome, aristocratic features grew saddened and pain pinched his long, straight nose.

Several men hastened to his call. They climbed to building tops only to cry out in despair. *"Los bandidos viene!* El Guillo and his bandits are coming! *Salvanos Dios!"*

"Yes," Padre Miguel thought somewhat bitterly. "'Save us Lord.' I'd feel better with a company of lancers around to rely on saving us."

Then the priest had to run for his church as El Guillo's men thundered into the village.

As usual, Tom Plaskoe was enjoying himself. He had a throbbing erection and visions of another good lay like Maria Elena swam in his red-hazed brain. He'd find another young, pretty one like her here in El Crucero and get the wench to suck him like his little sister used to do. Oh, that would be glorious. He saw three dark forms on one rooftop and had Manuel train the gun carriage upward.

A long stream of one inch bullets disintegrated adobe blocks into dusty clouds and the men sheltered behind them screamed and died. Pools of dark blood formed on the roof and seeped down through cracks to the inside.

"Hail Mary, full of grace . . ." Padre Miguel led his frightened flock in prayer. Women trembled and tears ran down their cheeks at the sounds of destruction and murder that came from outside. Children, the sobbing, wailing small ones watched over by the older, solemn boys and girls, crouched in the baptistry and behind the altar screen, in the confessionals and under the rude, hand-made wooden pew benches.

After a *decat* of *Aves*, he left his place on the ambulatory and walked out through the chancel rail gate. He crossed to the north trancept and peered out a window. In the distance, the big gun still boomed, writhed in demonic smoke, and its bullets trashed the fronts of yet another business. Already, Padre

97

Miguel noted with a pain in his chest, the grocery store had gone up in flames. Then the awful weapon fell silent and the whoops of barbaric bandits filled the street. They galloped about in a sort of frenzy for a while, seeking final resistors and silencing them with bullets in head or chest. Bitterness changed to anger, washing away pain and replacing it with fierce determination in the priest's breast.

A sudden silence came from outside. Only the crackle of flames could be heard. The women wailed in terror now, certain of their fate at the hands of the victorious bandidos. Children cried and even the oldest could not keep the hot, salty moisture from running down their pale cheeks. From all around the plaza came the sound of splintering wood and breaking glass while the bandits looted the town.

Damn them! Padre Miguel thought in unpriestly vehemence. "Damn them all to Hell!" he cried aloud. He felt helpless, stripped of his strength and, God forbid, nearly his faith. How could a kind and loving God permit such hideous slaughter and destruction? What purpose of the Blessed Christ was served by the murder of so many husbands and fathers? Had all sinned so blackly, as his Bishop would rationalize? And what of the women and older girls?

From stories of bandit raids of old, Padre Miguel well knew the fate planned for them by the brigands howling outside the church. His wrath grew mightily and he clinched his fists so tightly that the square-cut nails of his thick brown fingers dug into the palms until blood ran. He squeezed his eyes shut and cast his head back so that his face regarded heaven. A swift prayer rustled his lips as he asked for forgiveness for the thoughts and desires that burned in his mind. A cry from his aging sexton brought him out and through the nave to the front door.

"They're coming. Three of them, Padre."

"Inside the church," a harsh voice called from outside. "Open the doors, priest. This is El Guillo. Obey me and none shall come to harm."

Harsh laughter answered him from Padre Miguel. "Lying is a sin, O Prince of Liars. So long as strength remains in me, I shall not yield these women and children to your filthy designs."

"Come, let us be reasonable men, Padre," El Guillo countered. "We have the power to reduce your church to a pile of rubble. Will you sacrifice all for the sake of the church's gold?"

"That's what you want, is it? The only thing?"

"I promise you that it is. We take the gold and leave you alone."

Prompted by his calling and its devotion to good, Padre Miguel undid the bar over the small bolt-door in one huge portal. He stepped through it into the light. A swaggering El Guillo stood before him, chest puffed in triumph.

"It is good that you come out, priest. *Andele, muchachos*, strip the place. Bring out the gold and the women and girls."

"Stop! Do not enter this sanctuary. You said you wanted only the gold. That you would leave us alone."

"And we will . . . after we have our fill of your lovely women."

Rage more overpowering than all the strictures of Holy Mother Church overwhelmed Padre Miguel. With clawed hands, his only weapons, he leaped at El Guillo, intent on reaching his throat. "You son of a pig and a whore!"

Two of the bandits grabbed the priest in mid-jump and held him easily. "My, my, such language for a man of the cloth, Padre," El Guillo mildly chided. "You must be disciplined for that." He drew his big Colt Dragoon and cocked the hammer.

Even inside, the shot sounded like the clap of doom. Padre Miguel jerked once and fell from the grasp of El Guillo's henchmen, blood streaming from his head.

The sacking of the church began at once. The raping commenced only a short time later.

Through it all, Tom Plaskoe calmly sat on the tailboard of the carreta and cleaned his Gatling gun.

Maria Elena trembled in fright. She only too well recognized the sound of the big gun going off outside and, later, the sneering voice of El Guillo. She crouched in the "priest's hole," a secret hiding place and escape passage designed into every church since the earliest days of persecution of the faith. For a long while she huddled there, tears on her face for the horrid sounds that reached her ears.

Women and girls screamed and begged for mercy, though none was given. With the men of the village dead, a new generation would come only from those impregnated by the rude bandits who savaged their bodies. A ghastly sort of logic convinced the outlaws of the necessity of this. Without a fresh crop of males to grow up, who would work and store up and make this town worth raiding again? Muttered prayers rose and the scent of incense grew cloying. Three of the village girls, small for their age, shrieked their way to death as the brutal phalluses of the gang of desperadoes bludgeoned their tender parts to shreds and their lives ran out with their blood. All the while, Maria Elena remained silent and suffered in darkness.

Padre Miguel had shown her the refuge, complete with a tunnel, he had explained. She was to use it and if possible lead all she could to safety. When the attack came, she found she could not move. Terror held her tightly immobile. The stench of death and blood filled the air. Screams gradually turned to soft, despairing moans and at last to silence. The bandidos had left the church. Maria Elena strained to hear any sounds.

All her ears brought her were the sniffles and sobs of the small boys and littler girls, abandoned inside the desecrated nave. Two of the lads who served on the altar knew of the priest's hole and came to it as the sun sank low in the west. Maria Elena shrank back in horror and nearly made good her flight down the tunnel when they threw it open.

"*Señorita*," the older boy cried out. "You are safe. At least one woman of the village has been spared the shame."

"By the grace of God," the younger, a boy of eleven or so, added. "Please come out. We are all getting hungry and there is much sorrow and weeping. Someone must help. Someone strong."

Hesitantly Maria came from her hiding place. As had happened in her own village, the walls, altar and reliqueries had been stripped of all gold and precious stones. What had not been taken had been desecrated, overturned and dumped on the floor to be ground under the boots of the bandits. Blood smeared everywhere. Some of the bandits had satisfied their lust right in front of the door where she hid, in the presbytery before the high altar. A small, naked and helpless corpse lay there in a pool of red. Maria began to sob.

"A-re they gone?" she managed after a moment, while the solemn-faced little boys led her out of the nave.

"*Si*. For all of half an hour now. Be careful, *Señorita*, you must step over this ledge in the door."

Then Maria saw Padre Miguel. So young and kind, so solicitous of her fragile condition after two days on the high desert mountains. He had nursed her back to health and put her to helping around the church. He had been so kind, now he lay in a pool of blood. Her heart ached for his death.

Then, like a miracle, he groaned and moved feebly.

"He's alive!" she shouted. "Oh, Lupe, Diego, help me."

Maria and the two acolytes hurried to the downed priest. Unheeding his blood, she knelt and cradled his head. The wound, she discovered, had only been a crease along the side of his head. It bled profusely, but had not entered through the bone.

"Quickly. Go for water at the fountain, bring rags to bind Padre Miguel's head."

The boys scampered off, to return within a few minutes with a basin of water and some strips of white cotton cloth. Gently she ministered to the unconscious priest. He moaned again and one hand twitched. Once the ugly torn area had been bathed clean, she probed it gently, feeling a rush of joy that the head did not seem soft, as though the skull had shattered. Maria Elena bound the priest and remained with his head in her lap while she sent the boys to locate any of the women and girls who could stand and make do for cooking fires and a meal. Another half hour had nearly passed when Padre Miguel choked violently and began to struggle.

Maria calmed him and slowly his eyes opened. Clearly, they did not focus and she bent over him in concern. *"D-Dona Alicia. Mi amor. Yo te amo mucho,"* he gasped out in a feeble voice. He reached out hesitantly with one hand, as though he could as yet not see clearly.

Gently he stroked Maria Elena's cheek, then raised, lips puckered in a kiss. With a deep groan, he fell back into her arms. Consciousness fled from him again as she began to weep. A terrible insecurity fueled the flow of salt tears. She felt so alone and helpless. For all of her show of resourcefulness for small boys, she was frightened and didn't know what to do.

By mid-morning the following day, the fortunate few who had managed to flee the bandit raid had begun to return to El Crucero. Behind a small group of them rode Shelter Morgan and Raul Sanchez. Morgan's premonition that El Crucero would be a target for the bandits turned to reality as they trotted down the street and viewed the shot-up buildings.

Smoke still rose from two collapsed structures and the scent of death hung like a pall over the small village. In the plaza, the survivors gathered. An attractive young woman stood on the steps of the church and railed at them.

"You call yourselves men? Where were you when your wives, sisters and daughters were being raped by El Guillo's men? When Padre Miguel was shot? You ran and hid. You didn't even consider taking along those who should have been most precious to you. Your children stayed behind and witnessed it. *Tienes verguenza*, men of El Crucero. Have lots of shame upon you."

"What are we to do? We are not *soldados*. It is not our job to fight."

"Then whose is it?" the beautiful young woman shrieked back at them. "Your homes, your jobs, your wives and children despoiled by a pack of . . . of jackels and while some of your friends and relatives stayed and tried to prevent it, you ran with tails tucked tightly between your legs. Cowards! Who will fight if you do not?"

"We will," Shelter Morgan said quietly from the back of the crowd, after Raul had translated her words. He sat comfortably slouched in his saddle, though his hard gray-blue eyes moved ceaselessly, appraising the situation.

"Who are you?"

"I am called Raul Sanchez," El Tiburon prudently declared. He felt quite certain these people had heard and seen enough of bandidos for some time to come.

"I am Shelter Morgan, late of the Confederate States Army. If any among you will join us, we will seek these bandits and kill them all."

"Brave words," the girl on the steps jeered. "If you mean them. But among these . . . these rabbits, you will not find one with *cojones* enough to accept your offer, *Señor Gringo*."

"Don't be so quick to judge, miss," Shelter began, with Raul translating. "Give these men time to find themselves. If I am not mistaken, a powerful gun that fired rapidly many times without reloading was used in the attack, right?"

"How do you know this?" Maria Elena asked suspiciously.

"We are seeking the bandit leader known as El Guillo. In particular, I am after the American who owns and uses that gun. It is my intention to kill him. If El Guillo and his bandits get in the way, then they will also be killed."

A sudden smile lighted the girl's face and Shelter realized

how much more beautiful she was than he had previously considered. "You speak well. There is much to tell. Come, rest in our town, stay the night. Tomorrow you can ride on. Hopefully some of the men of El Crucero will find their lost courage and accompany you. I am called Maria Elena."

"Con mucha gusta, Señorita," Raul burbled enthusiastically for both of them.

12.

A cantina across the red, hard-packed earth plaza had escaped most of the destruction afforded the town. Maria Elena directed Shelter and Raul there and joined them shortly. Food was brought, along with tequila and small brown bottles of murky-white pulque.

"I am sorry there is no beer," Maria Elena apologized. "The bandidos drank it all or took it away with them."

Grinning, Raul hoisted a small terracotta cup of tequila. "The juice of the maguay is good enough for me, *bonita*."

"We have tortillas, *frijoles* and *cabrito*," the girl went on, ignoring Raul's coarse flirtation. "Do you, ah, like roast goat, *Señor Gringo*?" she asked Morgan. A faint hint of interest glowed deep in her eyes.

"I've had occasion to eat it before," Shelter replied, thinking of the days of near-starvation in those last fateful months of the War. "But never has it smelled so good."

"These are young. We do not eat the old billies," she told him through Raul. "It makes a lot of difference in taste."

Shelter's eyes fixed on hers, read them properly and he smiled. "I can tell you have excellent taste, *Señorita*."

"Please, call me Maria."

"I will, if you call me, Shell."

"Shell. It is an easy name for one who speaks Spanish to pronounce. I like that. Shell." She turned abruptly and shouted into the kitchen. "Guadalupe, hurry with the food. These gentlemen are starving."

A large plate appeared, borne by a tousel-headed, barefoot

child of eight or so. It contained some limp radishes, a mound of chopped onion, another of chili peppers, a cluster of cut limes and a clump of a green, pungent herb that Morgan did not recognize. A moment later, a fat, round-faced woman of indeterminate age, carried in a large platter heaped with steaming goat meat, crispy brown on the outside and moist gray within. She set it before the men and departed. Another youngster, a boy of ten or so, brought a woven basket of tortillas, covered by a square of cloth, and a bowl of powerful salsa. Morgan learned by watching.

Raul dug right in. He selected a hot tortilla, heaped chunks of cabrito into it, decorated that with onion, strips of chili and a radish. Over that he laced three pieces of the herb and squeezed a bit of lime juice atop that. Then he spooned on some of the fiery sauce from the bowl. He bit into it with gusto. Morgan followed his example, only he hesitated over the unknown green leaves.

"That is cilantro, *Señor* Morgan," Raul told him. "Very strong flavor, but it is good. Try some."

Shelter complied. He bit into the concoction and chewed appreciatively. It was superb! "This is delicious. Tell the cook I have never had anything quite like it."

"She will be pleased that you enjoy her food, Shell," Maria Elena responded. "Now, wash it down with a little pulque."

Shell did and winced at the slightly sour, fermented taste. Around him the watching staff, locals in for a meal, Maria Elena and Raul laughed. "It . . . it is different," Shell allowed.

After the meal, they talked, Maria Elena describing the events of the raid. Shell listened, fascinated by this recounting. How very like the stories he heard of the Yankee General, Sherman and his Bummers scourging Georgia. He and his men had seen the aftermath of that, including the beautiful spires of Atlanta reduced to smoldering rubble. Not much difference, he conceded, between El Guillo and his bandidos and the Yankees. Suddenly, in the midst of describing her exit from the priest's hole, Maria's face paled and she stared beyond Shelter

106

for a long instant.

"Padre Miguel, you should not be up and around as yet."
She rose and rushed toward the door.

"Now, now," a baritone voice answered smoothly. "I'm
quite all right, my child. Only a bad thump on the head. Why, I
can even see straight without my eyes crossing. By tomorrow, I
shall be fit as ever. We have visitors, I see," he went on,
including Shelter and Raul in the conversation.

"Yes, Padre." Maria made the introductions.

Padre Miguel studied Morgan closely. A fighting man, he
weighed. Yes, no doubt about it. A soldier at one time or
another. A leader at that.

"A *Norteamericano*, eh?"

"I am," Shell returned. Used to dubious looks from his
countrymen because of his obvious Southern origins, he
discovered that this new form of prejudice was more irritating
than the other.

"Welcome to El Crucero . . . what there is of it, *Señor*
Morgan. By your accent, I perceive that you are a Southerner."
Padre Miguel's English was flawless, if slightly accented.
"Many of the followers of your Cause joined with Mexico in
common effort against the usurpers of Maxmillian of Haps-
burg. You are most welcome here. I gather that you served the
Confederacy?"

"I did, sir. I was an officer in the Army of Northern Virginia
and later with the Army of Tennessee."

"To the bitter end, then?"

"Nearly so. I was captured a few days prior to the end of
hostilities."

"Again let me express how glad we are to have you here. It
seems we are in need of gallant men in El Crucero right now. I
don't wish to seem impolite, but could you enlighten us as to
your purpose in coming here?"

"We are on the trail of a man named Tom Plaskoe. He is a
criminal in my country and, it seems now, one in yours as
well."

"He is the man with the Gatling gun?"

"Yes. I think we have common cause now to go after him and El Guillo."

"Good!" Padre Miguel slapped his palms together. The unpriestlike vehemence startled Shelter.

"I, ah, understood that men of your calling were dedicated to peace and the love of God."

"That is so. But you will recall the trying times of the Middle Ages, the Baron Bishops and their armies of priestly knights?"

"I'm sorry, Padre, I never finished my schooling. Mine was a battlefield commission."

"I see. You are, nevertheless, an intelligent and resourceful man. The sort who might possibly succeed against El Guillo and his man with the Gatling." He sighed heavily. "We will talk more about this tomorrow. I fear I might have anticipated my recovery a bit. I must go back to the rectory and rest a while."

"Let me help you, Padre," Maria Elena offered.

Shelter and Raul spent the afternoon talking with the men remaining in El Crucero, attempting to recruit a strike force to go after the bandits. They met with singularly poor luck.

"*Hijo de la chingado!*" Raul swore in Spanish. He repeated i in English for Shelter's benefit. "Son of a beech. The girl was right. They have the hearts of rabbits. *Mierda!* More truly the hearts of mice. We have heard a million excuses, *amigo*, and every one of them so much bullsheet. You and I . . . we make a team. We are good together. Where do we find fighting men able to go against this great evil who can match us? Where?"

El Tiburon had been deeply moved by the plight of El Crucero. He had also been impressed by Shelter Morgan's reaction to it. He found he had come to admire the *gringo*. To actually *like* him. Gone were the thoughts of murdering him after the gold and gun had been secured. It would be, he considered in rejection, like killing his own brother. If doing things like El Guillo and his men did here—never had they been so bad when he had been in the gang—then perhaps being

108

a bandido was not such a good idea. He recalled, too, that it had been El Guillo who had cast him out. Who had allowed shameful things to be done to him as a small and helpless boy. It would be good to get revenge for these things. This Shelter Morgan could well be the means to do that.

For his own part, Shell felt this warming by Raul Sanchez. Subtle changes in attitude and his manner of address gave the hint that a lot of things had been rearranged in the would-be bandit's mind. He had a certain untrained courage. His sense of humor had been finely honed. Yet he remained an unknown factor. Although he had spoken freely during the journey of his life as a child, of once riding with El Guillo's bandits and of being cast out, there was a portion of his adult life that he never mentioned. Unaccounted years between being rejected by the bandits and arriving in Upper California as a bandit on his own. No matter. The years of privation during the War had taught Morgan to make do with what he had and El Tiburon apparently would be all he had. They returned to the cantina and ate an early supper.

"You seem miles away, Shell," Maria observed when she joined him after the meal.

"I was. Thinking of where El Guillo and his gang went from here. Of how I can get close enough to Tom Plaskoe to kill him."

"Such violent thoughts!" Maria Elena exclaimed.

"I'm sorry. Would you like to go for a walk? Show me more of your town?"

"It is not my home. I was taken from La Rumorosa by El Guillo a month ago. I escaped though." A look of triumph came into her eyes while Raul translated. "I know where his hideout is. I climbed a cliff to get away and none could come after me."

"Where is this?" Excitement colored Shell's words so that it was not even necessary for Raul to turn them into Spanish.

"A small cove, land-locked, at the southern end of Bahia de Los Angeles."

"We could not get there by land?"

"It is most difficult. And you would have to be on foot. It is better, I think, to catch them somewhere else."

Silence held while Morgan digested this exciting news. "Enough of this talk of bandits. What about that walk?"

"Oh, yes. I would be most happy."

They rose to go and Raul looked expectantly at the American. "Shouldn't I go along to interpret?"

Shell smiled at him. "No. This time I don't think we'll have any language barrier."

"*Por Dios!* It's that way, is it? You are *un macho hombre,* Shel-tor."

"*Gracias,*" Shell replied in one of the more polite words of Spanish he had picked up since he first arrived in San Diego two weeks earlier.

A fat half-moon hung in the sky and shed muted silver light on the rubble of El Crucero. Most of the homes had not been damaged and the residents had taken to their dwellings for the night. Maria Elena led Shell out to the south of town.

"There's a small spring near here," she told him in her language. "I thought you would like to see it."

"You're lovely, did you know that?" he asked in his.

Maria Elena smiled. The words sounded so sweet, no matter their meaning.

A long walk brought them to the secluded grassy bowl that contained the spring. Willows and live oak grew there, spreading a wide canopy that blotted out the stars and moon. They paused on the bank of a small pool and Maria Elena pointed with her hand.

"See. The spring. Before wells were dug in El Crucero, the people must have come here for their water. It is sweet and fresh. Padre Miguel told me about it."

Shelter could make no sense of her words, though the heat radiating from his loins carried a message clear enough to read. He reached out and took her in his arms. She came to him readily, lips pursed for the kiss that he gave her.

Gentle at first, their lips grew warm and active, writhing

110

snakes that told in a universal language of the needs and desires of each. Maria's tongue parted Shell's lips and probed along the hard line of his white, even teeth and healthy pink gums. She pressed her body against his, thrilling to the rigid pressure of his expanded organ. He opened wide and swallowed her flexing tongue. It found his own and they conducted a fencing match of mounting passion. When the embrace ended, Maria helped him remove her clothing.

She lay her shawl on the soft turf and turned to him. Tiny rays of moonlight filtered through the leaves, mottling her luscious brown body with highlights that tantalized. Her firm young breasts stood proudly upright, dark circles backgrounding her large, spongy nipples. Shell breathed deeply and hurriedly undressed.

"*Ay! Muy grande!*" Maria Elena exclaimed when his long, rigid phallus swung into view. The shaft curved upward slightly, stretched and strained by its excitement so that the large, flat tip shown in the soft light. She stepped toward him and reached out to encompass it with her trembling fingers. Its thickness thrilled her and she wondered if she could ever hope to exhaust the *grande caballero* in the manner she had used on El Guillo. Not likely. Not she and all the girls in El Rumorosa working in shifts.

"Shell . . . *ay* . . . Shell," she exhaled in a delighted sigh. Slowly she began to stroke him. *Dios!* He is like a great stallion.

As though he had caught her thoughts, Shelter shuddered like a stallion suddenly brought to stud with a quickened and ready mare. Maria Elena dropped to her knees, lips and tongue teasing the expanse of his turgid tip while her one hand cupped the large sack beneath and the other continued to tug at the shaft, sending sensations of ecstacy through his body. At least, she thought mischieviously, she could try.

When his peak came and Maria Elena did not release him for even an instant, Shelter experienced such intense pleasure that his knees weakened. He sagged downward, Maria following until she lay on her belly on the shawl, her mouth

111

never relinquishing an inch of his swollen tool. He gasped in delighted disbelief as she continued to send jolts through his sturdy frame, maintaining his magnificent erection with skill that denoted great practice.

Fireworks exploded in his head a second and incredibly a third time and still she would not desist from her eager, hungry suction that forced more and more of him into her greedy mouth. If this went on much longer, he realized, he could not bear it. Firmly he extricated his throbbing penis and eased her onto her side.

Shell lay beside her, their bodies touching in many places. Her firm breasts formed spots of wildly stimulating warmth on his chest as he elevated her left leg and inched forward until the fiery brand that thrust out from his pelvis contacted the moist, burning folds of her portal of enchantment. She reached for him and helped to slather that mighty member in nature's slick juices, then gently eased barely the first inch into that silken cleft. There she inscribed spirals, teasing herself as her tongue had done this raging lance. Her breath broke into gasps and of themselves, her hips began to undulate.

With a mighty heave, Shell thrust forward. A small shriek came from Maria Elena and she adjusted his trajectory so that he plunged far into her pulsating pantry. She looked down the length of his muscular, scarred body and, with a shock, discovered that only half of that iron rod had penetrated her passage. How full she felt, yet every bit as much more remained to pierce her.

"Soy listo," she panted. *"Darme el todo!"*

Shell had been right. He needed no interpreter. With a powerful shove he gave her all of it as she had asked. It was like forcing his organ through the powerful grip of a silken vice.

Fire and ice! Maria Elena felt as though she had been split asunder by that mighty weapon. Never had she expanded her passage so widely to accommodate any man. *Ay!* A stallion indeed. His ponderous appendage made her feel like a virgin again. *Muy guapo! Muy macho!* she exulted. Drained three times and he came at her with the freshness of a youth on his first conquest. She trembled all over and clung to him, legs wrapped around his waist now, thrilling to the powerful surges of his body as he slid that immensity in and out of her aching, quivering tunnel. *Perfectamente!* Absolutely perfect. It made all the others seem like little boys who barely knew how to jerk their *vergas*, let alone do proper service for a woman. Incredibly she felt herself racing up the incline to an explosive and masterful release.

Blam! . . . Blam! . . . Blam! Like a monstrous cannon she climaxed amid squeals of irrational joy. On he surged, carrying her along before she could even relax from the cataclysmic fulfillment he had just given her. They rolled until she lay on her back, legs high in the air, kicking in spasms of her entrancing oblivion. His surges became more powerful, longer, driving deep into her inner core, withdrawing with a stupendous burst of sensation while he ground his hips in a circle. Then down, down again until she thought her womb would be transfixed with his hugeness.

By the time his own completion came, they had become delirious on the heady scents of their passion and stimulated beyond human endurance by the friction of love.

"Oh God," he cried out. "Oh . . . God . . . YES!"

They walked back to town hand-in-hand, silent and content. Shell felt light-headed, empty, yet fuller than ever before. Maria Elena buzzed and tingled all over. She thought idly of entering the church. Never would there be another man like this. She would rather give herself to the service of God than to settle for second best.

"You . . . managed to communicate without me?" Raul asked when Shelter entered the small house they had been given for quarters.

The soft gaze in Morgan's gray-blue eyes and the sappy smile on his face provided an answer that made the amateur bandido giggle.

El Arco shimmered in the sun. Tom Plaskoe didn't like mid-

113

day attacks. The heat caused objects to waver and become indistinct in the broiling air. All the same, they would have been discovered and the village alerted had they waited. He grasped the crank of the Gatling and began to turn.

Turmoil erupted in El Arco. Adobe burst into puffs of dust, splatters of blood sprayed from ruptured bodies and coated the whitewashed plaster of building fronts. Women screamed and children ran shrieking in fright. Horses broke from the tierail in front of the only cantina, to collapse in mid-stride and fall in a welter of crimson and spilled intestines. Resistance stiffened a moment and then fell apart under the howls of El Guillo's charging outlaws.

In ten minutes the main street had been sieved by one inch shells and two buildings blazed. Quickly the available money, jewelry and reserve gold from the small bank transferred to saddle bags. A wagon clattered to a stop in front of the cantina. Bandits swarmed around it, loading barrels of beer, wooden cases of tequila and brandy, crockery jugs of mescal and pulque. One desperado invaded a small *putaria* attached to the cantina and came out wrapped in a feather boa and the long red, feather-trimmed lounging robe of one of the whores.

"*Oye! Mira te.* Look at me," he repeated. "I am very beautiful, no?"

A trio of bandidos stopped work, laughed and slapped their thighs. "What is the *puta* wearing?"

"Only her golden skin, *amigos*. Only her skin. Such nice skin it is."

"They are hard-working, honest girls," El Guillo growled. "We leave them alone. Return that, Fernando, and pay the girl twenty gold pesos for your rudeness."

"*Si, jefe.* But . . . twenty gold pesos. That's a lot of money."

"Hurry, you dog. We have the women to get from the church and the gold to take."

A poor church, in a small, poor village, San Sabastian yielded up little gold or jewels for the growing horde of loot. The raping proved even less satisfying. Only a handful of old

114

women, toothless crones hardly worth the effort. Surly and unsatisfied, the men began a search.

"*Vien . . . vien!*" one burly outlaw shouted a short time later. He gleefully pointed out a haystack to his companions. "The tender young ones of El Arco are hiding there."

Shrewder than the others, Tom Plaskoe had gone a roundabout way to slake his lust. He had prowled the cluster of houses around the central plaza, peeking into windows and doorways. Soon he found what he sought.

"Come out, little one," he purred to a big-eyed girl in a faded, well-worn dress that didn't come to her knees. "Yes. You'll do nicely."

She whimpered once when he fastened his fingers around her thin upper arm, then went along willingly enough, scuffing her bare toes in the dirt. Plaskoe took her to the wagon. His heart thudded with anticipation. Already his rigid penis ached to be released from the restraint of his trousers and longjohns. The young girl gazed at the bulge in the front of his whipcords and a winsome smile, which Plaskoe didn't see, formed on her lips. He hoisted her slight figure into the carreta and quickly joined her.

He whipped her dress off over her head and found her completely naked beneath it. Tiny, newly formed breasts jutted out at him. Pale pink, they looked totally untouched to him. Not a single strand of hair covered her chubby little mound and the sight of it caused him to suck in a breath.

"*Como se llama, niña?*" he gasped out.

"I am called Violeta. I have thirteen years and have just gone to work for . . ."

Eager now, Plaskoe interrupted her. "Never mind that. I am called Tomas. I want to be your friend." With trembling fingers he reached out and gently stroked her cleft. To his surprise, he found it moist and yielding. "Do you like that?"

Violeta giggled. "Oh, yes. It feels funny." She thrust her pelvis forward and drove two fingers into the wet fronds that shaded her portal.

115

"Gaagh," Plaskoe stammered. The ache in his loins nearly doubled him over and he grew worried that he would explode in his pants if he didn't hurry. Quickly he removed his trousers and bottom half of his longjohns. His small penis swung upward and quivered like a good hunting dog on point.

Instantly, Violeta pounced on it. She began tugging rapidly with a firm and skillful fist. Plaskoe slid his fingers deeper into her little furnace and, with his thumb, began to rub the rigid protrusion encased at the top of her crevice. Violeta wriggled and licked dry lips to a bright sheen. Her slender hips, only beginning to widen to womanliness, began to undulate, driving his digits further into her burning tunnel.

"Hurry, Tomas," she pleaded. "Fuck me. Fuck me hard."

Tom Paskoe blinked his eyes. He couldn't believe what he had heard. This was better than when he was a boy! Violeta pressed her face against his bare belly and began to lick him. Her soft black hair tickled and waves of electric delight spread from her tongue. Before he could touch her, she lay down and spread her legs wide.

"Now, Tomas. Please do it now."

Eagerly, Tom complied. He thrust deeply and violently into the little girl. She squealed and wiggled beneath him, driving upward to meet his shove. Unbelievable, Tom thought wildly. He'd truly found paradise.

Young and energetic, a regular bedroom gymnast of vast experience, Violeta quickly brought Plaskoe to his peak. With only a moment's respite, the tiny wanton began to thrust herself against him again, talented muscles pumping him to full rigidity while they clasped his small member inside with no avenue of escape. Tom responded.

After the second time, past experience told him, he should have his choice sobbing for mercy. Violeta only begged for more.

When he spurted to completion the third time, it was he who wanted to cry for succor. Weak and limp from his exertion, he could only sigh with relief when Violeta relinquished her tight grip and let him withdraw. His reddened, sore manhood drooped, though not for long. Violeta's mouth closed over it and she began to run her tongue in spirals over his already tingling tip. Bright lights exploded behind his eyes and his body roused to even more shafts of joyous stimulation.

Plaskoe panted and sagged by the time Violeta finished her massage with lips and tongue. "No more. Please no more," he begged. "You . . . you wore me out."

"I can see why," Violeta snapped scornfully. "That tiny little thing. I've seen bigger on babies. Even the little boys who come for their first time to the *putaria* where I work have *chiles* longer than that."

"What did you say?" Plaskoe's voice had turned to ice.

Violent, horrified screams drew El Guillo and a dozen of his bandits from the cantina where they amused themselves with drink and women. They rushed out into the plaza to see Tom Plaskoe standing before the large stone cross at the center of the square. He appeared to be tying something to it. When he completed his work he stepped back. A young, naked girl, eyes wide with terror, hung there, trembling with her efforts to escape. Plaskoe trotted away from his handywork and climbed into the wagon box of his carreta, which he had driven close into the village. All the while Violeta continued to shriek.

"What are you doing, *amigo*?" El Guillo called after him.

"She . . . she made fun of me. Said my pecker was too small. Said I couldn't keep it up as good as a little boy. I'll show her."

His hand reached out and began to crank the handle of the Gatling gun.

The big 1.1 inch slugs literally exploded her body, splattering bits and pieces of the helpless young girl over the square, gouging out large chunks of the stone cross and splattering the astounded and sickened bandidos with dollops of her gore. The huge bullets ended Violeta's cries for mercy.

13.

The church bell, though damaged, awakened Shelter Morgan the next morning with its rich-voiced tolling. Padre Miguel had mended well. He held an early Mass, one of thanksgiving for those who survived and of requiem for those who did not. Afterward he joined Shelter, Raul and Maria Elena for breakfast.

"Apparently those bandidos did not have a taste for *chorizo*. They left an entire string of it hanging in the rectory kitchen," the priest announced, displaying a long rope made of red-brown bulges. "I brought it along for breakfast. It will feed many besides ourselves."

While Guadalupe, the fat cook at the cantina prepared the meal, the subject turned to Shelter's plans.

"I figured to ride out of here today. Before the trail gets cold, I would like to get close enough to study this El Guillo and learn how they go about picking targets, how effective their men are. Once I have done this I can decide how and where to attack them."

"Excellent strategy, *Señor* Morgan," Padre Miguel declared. "Even once you determine this, you will need more than the two of you to fight the bandits, is that not so?"

"True, Padre," Shell agreed. "I am hoping that you will be able to inspire some of the men in this town to go after El Guillo when the time comes."

"They are like frightened children. Unless they see with their own eyes, and know in their hearts that the bandits can be defeated, they will not believe. And that they won't do because

118

they are afraid. It would be better if I went with you, then reported back to them. They would have to believe what I said."

"No, Padre," Maria Elena protested. "You have been wounded."

"It would be dangerous, sir," Shelter added.

"Danger is of no consequence to me."

"Maria Elena is right about your wound," Shell pressed.

"I insist. I must go or you will have no help when you need it. Besides, I sent Juan to the *Hacienda* Bustamante for a horse. He returned an hour before sunrise."

"No disrespect, Padre," Raul began in a light tone Shell well recognized. "But . . . can you do this?" The would-be *bandido* rose from his chair and walked out of the cantina. The others followed.

In the street, Raul drew his Smith and Wesson .44 and took aim on the fallen sign of the burned-out grocery store. He cocked and fired five rounds, taking only scant time between shots to aim. With him in the lead, the other three went forward to inspect his marksmanship.

Three holes showed in the open space of the "O" in *ABAROTES*. Two more of them touched the black paint on the right side.

"That is good shooting, my son," the priest remarked. "Permit me?" he asked of Shell.

Together the quartet walked back to the designated firing line. Padre Miguel raised Morgan's Colt and cocked the hammer. Quickly he discharged five shots.

Two large holes appeared in the top portion of the first "A."

"Three misses, Padre," Raul announced somewhat smugly.

"Let's go see," the priest suggested. He noticed a slight smile on Shelter Morgan's face.

At the sign, four heads bent low to examine the shot-up letter. Two slugs had cut holes closely enough to create a figure-eight. A large chunk of wood had been chewed out in a rough triangle also. Behind it were three bullet holes in the adobe. None of the rounds had touched the black paint.

"Jesus, Mary and Joseph!" Raul exclaimed. "That shooting took a miracle, Padre."

"Not really," Padre Miguel explained. "You see, my son, before I had a call to take Holy Orders, I was *Capitan* Miguel Espinosa of the Fourth Lancers in the Army of Mexico."

Raul blinked and turned pale. His reaction brought a curious frown to the foreheads of Padre Miguel and Shelter Morgan. *"Todos Santos!"* the bandit exclaimed.

"If my memory serves me correctly, Raul Manuel Sanchez y Hertado was the name of a young, frightened recruit who deserted the Fourth Lancers in the face of the enemy during a battle with the French in 'Sixty-four."

"I . . . I—I—I . . ." For the first time since his humiliation in the streets of Julian, all the wind went out of Raul. He shrank from the gaze of the others and seemed to grow smaller. Shame blazed from his face.

"I regret to say, Padre, that your memory does not fail you. I am that Raul Manuel Sanchez y Hertado. I am ashamed of what I did. I was young, frightened. I ran. I am sorry and wish to take my punishment."

"Then . . ." Shelter began, putting things together in his head, "what you told me about riding with El Guillo was not true?"

"Oh, El Guillo is one I know only too well. He took me from the village of my birth at an early age. My father and mother had been killed in the bandit raid. What I said about being abused and badly used as a small boy was true. There were two, perhaps three, men in the camp who did not care particularly if they held a girl or a boy in their arms when the need came upon them. I was available." He shrugged. "I was used. Until El Guillo learned of this unmanly practice and put an end to it by shooting them. After that, it wasn't so bad. Although, I never rode with him.

"When I reached my fourteenth year, I ran away. Stole one

120

of the bandido's horses and ran for my life. I . . . I wanted to atone for my past. I decided to join Juarez in the fight against Maxmillian and the French. I went into the army. Then, after I did this cowardly deed by deserting my comrades I felt such shame, I . . . I made up a new life for myself. Hid the truth from all eyes, including my own. I came to believe it. In truth, I have not ever wanted to be a bandido. I went north to *Los Estados Unidos*. I herded sheep in New Mexico, cattle in Texas. Then I went to California. Of late things have not done well. So, I decided to try the only other thing I had any training for." He looked shyly at Shelter Morgan.

"I really wasn't a very good bandido, was I?"

"No. But in my book, you're one hell of a man, El Tiburon."

"*Muchas gracias.*" Unshed tears shined in Raul's eyes.

Padre Miguel cleared his throat. "There is still the matter of this desertion to deal with." Raul's face fell. "To which I shall address myself now. Taking into consideration that there are no facilities for a proper court martial and hanging . . ." Raul winced at the word. "And the life of an outcast and a bandido is far more hazardous than that of a soldier, I feel that this certain young man, Raul Manuel Sanchez y Hertado has redeemed himself. That his acts have been forgiven by man and by God. Wherever this man might be, I would suggest he go to the nearest church, make a good act of contrition, say a decat of Hail Mary's and try to live up to the image others now have of him."

"B-bless you, Padre," Raul nearly blubbered. He hurried away with no one needing to ask where he headed.

"Now, as to my going along . . . ?"

"Uh . . . yes. Yes, I think that might be advisable, Padre. Or should I call you Captain?"

"Either one, Mister Morgan. You'll excuse me. I have to see to cleaning and oiling my old revolver."

"Better pick one of the new cartridge models, Padre," Morgan suggested.

121

"I figure to do that off of one of El Guillo's bandits."

They met at the spring, when the moon stood only an hour high over the horizon. Shelter brought a blanket. The cool mountain air had chilled them both the night before. Swiftly they removed their clothes and embraced. Shelter's manhood swelled rapidly and pressed insistently into the warm, soft flesh of Maria Elena's abdomen. When their kiss ended, Maria asked hesitantly.

"When you have located the bandidos, will you come back?"

"Yes."

"Then what?"

"If we have enough men willing to fight, we'll attack them."

"After that will you come back to me?"

"I . . ." Shell started to lie, to say he would. All of a sudden he found himself wanting to. Maria was really some lady. He knew, though, that he could not. He had to go on until every last man paid for his treachery. "I want to very much. But, I have something to do. A mission."

Her voice turned cold, brittle. "Of vengeance."

"Yes." Shelter had strained, then exhausted his scant knowledge of Spanish and only floundered to make meaning of her words.

"Is that all there is for you men? Killing and revenge and more killing. Always fighting, and why? Because it is *macho*. Guns . . . knives . . . oh, God, I wish they had never been invented." She flung herself against him and began to sob, hot tears wetting his bare chest.

"It would make little difference *chiquita*," Shell murmured sadly. "Sticks and stones will serve if they are all that's available."

Morgan gently lifted her and laid her on the blanket, then lowered himself beside her and covered them both. She continued to cry and make small whimpering sounds. A long time passed before passion stirred in either of them.

"There is so little time. So little," Maria Elena whispered as she searched out his flaccid organ and began to work it to life. "Love me now. Love me while we still can."

Shelter quickly responded, heat surging from his loins. He entered her slowly, deeply. Then they began to rock in the rhythm of eternity.

At Padre Miguel's suggestion they took another burro for pack duty. The survivors of El Crucero, led by Maria Elena, turned out early the next morning to see the trio off. She cried, as did many of the women. The children glowed with pride to see their priest, garbed in his brown Franciscan robe, white tie-cord hidden by the wide leather of a military pistol belt, astride a blooded horse and ready for battle. The few men slunk at the rear of the gathering, shame-faced. This warrior-priest represented an unbearable assault on their image of *macho*.

Their time would come, they promised themselves silently. Only first let them rebuild, strengthen their village, bury the dead and start life over. Then, oh yes, then they would strike down the oppressors. Only one, a young man named Andres Bargas, saddled his shaggy-coated horse and galloped out of town to join the expedition.

"Why have you changed your mind and decided to come, my son?" Padre Miguel asked him when he reached the others.

"You showed us our shame, Padre. More than that, I am doing it for Isabel. She . . . she was soiled by those *cabrones*. It is my duty to avenge her. Then he added simply. "Also I still have a horse because I rode out of town like the rabbit Maria called me."

"Spoken like a true *caballero*," Raul Sanchez praised the youth. He felt a new man, as though some unbearable weight had been lifted from his shoulders. He rode with heroes and, like the young man Andres, he did so because he wanted to.

The morning remained bright and warm as they rode

through the rugged countryside. Behind them, though, far to the southwest, the air turned opaque with haze, masking a towering, angry cell of clouds that swirled in counter-clockwise direction as it moved toward the Pacific coast of Baja California. The four searchers reached El Arco late in the afternoon.

Andres Bargas made gagging sounds and lost his noon meal of cold beans and tortillas as the quartet grimly viewed the remains of a young girl hung on the cross at the center of the plaza. Raul Sanchez turned away, fires of savage hatred burning in his eyes. Shelter Morgan swallowed to push down his own rising nausea, then scanned the savaged buildings around the square.

"'May the Lord Jesus Christ have mercy on you,'" Padre Miguel chanted in Latin as he made the sign of the cross with his extended arm in final benediction for the unfortunate girl eyes fixed on the grisly sight. The poor little child, he wondered. What had she done to deserve this?"

"That was done with the Gatling gun," Morgan advised them. "See the damage to the cross?"

"W-why hasn't she been taken down?" Andres managed to get out.

"I don't think there is anyone left alive here," Padre Miguel answered him.

"We'll bury her," Shelter decided, "and ride on."

At Las Arrastas, two days later, they again arrived too late. Smoke still rose from collapsed buildings and the scent of death hung heavily over the sprawled corpses in the streets and buildings. A few dirty, haunted-eyed children crawled from the rubble and begged them pitifully for food and to tell them where their parents had gone.

"Find enough of something to fix a big meal for these kids," Shell ordered. "We can't move too far before morning. Padre can you care for their cuts and bruises? Whatever else you can

124

do? Tell Andres I want him to scout the trail for an hour's ride from the village, then return. We're getting closer," he finished grimly.

Not close enough, they discovered the next day. The trail led in a wide, curving path of destruction and butchery. The four avengers reached Calamajue a few minutes short of nightfall. Here the destruction had been complete. Not a soul had survived. On the next day, Gonzaga and after that, Alfonsina fell in rapid succession. With each passing moment, bitterness, anger and iron determination to destroy all these scum fashioned a bond between Shelter Morgan and his three companions. If only they could catch up.

Screams, moans and muttered prayers rose from behind the convent walls of the Sisters of Charity at Mission Santa Maria. Lust-crazed bandits swaggered the halls, bottles of precious sacramental wine in their hands, seeking more of the gentle nuns who had not died or had hidden from the atrocities. As the day wore on, acts of unspeakable horror became commonplace to the cloistered women. The brutish animals who rutted on them over and over could not be dissuaded by any appeal.

Only Christ could, in His mercy, release them from their suffering and martyrdom. Except, Christ didn't seem to be listening at the time. Some of the nuns were roused from their degradation to prepare a meal.

"Make it a good one," El Guillo commanded in a liquor-harshened voice. "You've got turkeys here. Do us a *mole*. And those suckling pigs across the road. Let's have them on a spit. Hurry, damn you," he growled at the Mother Superior.

"God shall bring His wrath down on you for this," the aging Mother Superior promised with a shaking fist.

"El Guillo fears neither man nor God. Now be quick about it, old woman."

"Blasphemer! Heretic! Barbarian scum. You will pay. Mark my words on that!"

El Guillo took a menacing step toward her, one hand on the hilt of a large knife in his belt. "Watch that mouth of yours, or I cut off a tit and stuff it in as a gag."

So lustful and violent grew the depredations of the bandit horde that they failed to hear the silent approach of four grim men.

"Andres, they have left a single guard at the gate to the convent," Padre Miguel translated Shelter's words in a voice shaking with fury. "Take him out silently and then signal us. Go in and bar the gate from inside. We'll come through the garden port."

"Yes, Padre."

"Give no quarter," the priest added to Morgan's instructions. As he, Raul and Shelter waited for the signal, Miguel began to hum a haunting tune barely audible to the others. Its harmony raised the hackles on Shelter Morgan's neck.

"What is that Padre Miguel is humming?" he asked Raul in a whisper.

"The *Diguello*. The no quarter song. Santa Anna ordered it played at the, ah, the Alamo."

"And much more fitting for these bastards, *verdad*?" the priest broke off to add.

"Indeed," Shelter agreed crisply. "Too bad we don't have a band along to serenade them with it."

"As it happens, Andres brought his trumpet along. If we don't finish it here, we'll have him try it on them next time," Padre Miguel informed the ex-Confederate.

"Remember, we go for the Gatling gun. With that in our hands, it will be a slaughter."

"*Si, Señor* Morgan," Miguel agreed. "Only my first duty is to see to the safety of the Sisters. That will involve considerable shooting I'm afraid. With Andres at the gate, that leaves only two of you to man the gun. Can you do it?"

"It can be operated by one man, only slowly," Shelter

informed him, recalling what he knew from past encounters with the awesome weapons. Shelter's eyes narrowed as he watched the shadowy figure of Andres Bargas slip up behind the sentry.

A loop of rope dropped over the bandido's neck. A quick jerk, twist and turn. Andres bent forward, drawing the victim off his feet. The garotte bit into flesh. The guard died silently kicking the air. Andres released him and waved his hand.

"Let's go."

Padre Miguel and Raul followed Morgan's command. They hurried through tall grass to a sidewall of the compound. There a small gate hung open. Cautiously they neared this goal and paused. A quick check showed no one close to the opposite side. With Shelter Morgan in the lead, the trio entered.

Two bandits surprised them as they divided to go about their assigned tasks. Shelter's Bowie knife hissed through the air and opened the belly of the nearest. His dark, slithery intestines spilled onto the ground, robbing him of the strength to yell, and Morgan jumped backward to avoid the gusher of blood that accompanied them. The second man's eyes widened and he opened his mouth to shout a warning.

Raul's machete flashed in dim afternoon light and made a meaty, butchershop sound as it struck flesh. The bandido's head flew from his shoulders before he managed a single word. Twin geysers of orange-red spurted into the air, while darker red fountained from his severed veins.

"Go find the women, Padre," Shelter said, tight-lipped.

Gunfire erupted in the direction of the front entrance. Shouts of surprise and consternation rose from all quarters. Bandits began to rush about in every direction. Three of them ran blindly toward Padre Miguel.

"It's nothing but a priest," the lead man said in disgust when he saw the clerical robe.

"What the hell. Gun him down anyway," another advised.

Padre Miguel turned and took careful aim. The unexpected appearance of the weapon in his hand caused the bandits to check their charge. The former Lancer captain cooly shot the first between the eyes. He cocked his percussion revolver again and downed a second before the remaining one could react. He ran.

A fatal mistake.

Padre Miguel lined up the sights of his Mexican copy of the 1860 Colt .44 and drilled a ball between the outlaw's shoulder blades.

Five more tried their luck on Shelter and Raul. Three died before the others decided to seek escape elsewhere. So far, Shelter had not seen the Gatling gun. He looked about for the carreta described in El Crucero but saw nothing of it. Heavier fire came from the area of the main gate.

Andres shot down two bandits and turned toward a third. A hot pain bloomed in his left shoulder and the force of the bullet slammed him back against the gate. Six bandidos charged him then, and a rifle butt slammed against his head. He went down, deep into blackness, while the panicked brigands clawed at the locking bar and flung the gates wide in search of escape.

Shelter Morgan lined his sights on a tall, big-bellied bandit with a flowing mustache and huge, gold-embroidered sombrero. The hair-rimmed mouth opened wide, deep voice bellowing orders. It had to be El Guillo.

Cut off the head and the body dies, Morgan thought as he squeezed the trigger.

Another bandido, mounted, rode between the Winchester's muzzle and the intended target. The .44-40 crashed and the heavy slug cleaned the Mexican gunman from his saddle. In a whirl of confusion El Guillo disappeared into dust, smoke and shouting men.

Morgan threw a snap-shot at another fleeing outlaw. "It's not here," he yelled over the tumult to Raul. "Plaskoe took it away before we came. All we can do is roust the rest of these rats out of their lairs."

In two minutes the fighting ended. Padre Miguel, now armed with a fairly new, good condition .45 Colt, comforted the rescued nuns while Shelter and Raul cared for the wounded youth from El Crucero.

"It is not a bad wound," Raul observed. "Went through clean. He will survive."

Andres groaned and blinked his eyes.

"Can you move your left arm?" Morgan asked him.

"Yes. See it is . . . ow! It hurts. So does my head."

"They will for a while. You've been shot and clubbed with a rifle."

Unseen, a wounded bandido painfully forced himself upright in a small cubical where he had been raping a nun when the fighting started. He tightly clutched his *pistola* and staggered to the doorway. Fighting a world that swirled around him from blood loss and the weakness of his legs, he raised the revolver into place.

A large clay olla shattered six inches above Raul's head and showered him with cool water, its breaking lost in the report of the bandit's six-gun. Before Raul could react, Shelter had rolled forward to his right and came up in a sitting position. The .45 Colt in his hand spit fire and a 255 grain slug smashed in the chest of the wounded outlaw.

He flew backward and smacked into the doorpost. A thick smear of red followed him downward, painting gore on the white plastered wall.

"Nice shooting, Shel-tor my *amigo*" Raul gasped.

"Thanks. But not enough of them. Not nearly enough."

14.

Shelter and his three man force pursued the bandits until sundown. A dozen rode in one cluster, the rest had scattered in all directions. Morgan speculated on whether it had been a preplanned maneuver or simple confusion as a result of the unexpected attack. Whatever the case, signs of the enemy grew thinner, tracks faded out until they seemed to disappear into smoke. Darkness halted the search.

After an hour's ride into the next morning, all sign of the trail ceased. Shelter announced that they would split up and work a wide arc in all four directions. At Padre Miguel's suggestion, the rendezvous point would be a canyon that held a passable stream, half a day ahead.

Shelter ranged out, making wide zig-zags across his area. He found nothing. By noon, the wind had come up and huge towers of dark clouds filled the western sky. A sudden chill descended. So gigantic was the roiling mass that Morgan had no way of estimating how far off it might be. He shrugged into a jacket and rode on.

A light rain squall washed over him an hour later. It lasted only a short while and raced on across the sere mountains. Another, he noticed, came scudding up out of the southwest. He put spurs to his mount and the big black responded willingly.

He made good time, though the storm caught up to drench him a good hour before he estimated he would reach the protection afforded by the canyon. A quiet, unearthly calm followed the speeding shower. The thirsty ground had not yet absorbed its fill, but mud puddles had formed in many shallow depressions. Progress slowed. Shelter chaffed at the delay and silently cursed the rain. Any scant sign of the bandits' trail would be destroyed. Ahead of him an apparently solid mountain ridge revealed a fold that slowly defined itself as the canyon described by Padre Miguel.

Shelter found he had reached the spot first. He set about locating a good campsite. A few feet above the creekbed, he found a shelf, with a large overhang that would provide a haven in the event of more rain. Grass grew in plenty along the stream and the water was sweet and potable. Shelter picketed his horse and the one packmule and began to unload.

The cooking gear came first. He located a spot and set up the tripod, built a large ring of stones to contain the fire, then went to collect windfall wood. He had his arms loaded for the fifth time, half an hour later, when he heard the clop of approaching hoofs.

Andres Bargas entered the canyon and rode to where Shelter's animals grazed. He saw the American coming and set to collecting more wood without instructions. Shelter took advantage of the extra help to take time to kindle a fire. The air turned thick and humid, though the temperature took another drastic drop, before Padre Miguel and Raul Sanchez rode in together.

"Would that be coffee I smell cooking?" the priest asked jovially.

"That it is," Shell told him.

Padre Miguel dismounted and Raul took the reins of his horse. He stood with hands on hips and looked around, glancing lastly at the sky.

"I do not like what I see above us," the priest announced.

"What is it, Padre? A thunderstorm?"

"Worse than that, my friend," Miguel told Shelter. "It could well be one of the terrible hurricanes that strike this peninsula. God grant that it is not. Or if it is, that it misses us."

He had hardly spoken the words when a huge blackness

engulfed the light overcast above them. Giant banks of roiling clouds swirled and buffeted each other and torrents of rain began to fall. In the distance, deflected and distorted by the canyon walls, a roar that Shelter thought similar to a runaway locomotive grew in violence. Without warning the wind whipped to gale force and rattled the leaves on the cottonwoods along the stream. Long, brittle branches tore from willows and went streaming in the blast.

Inexorably, the roaring grew closer. The tempest increased and oily rivulets of mud began to wash down the canyon walls. A moment later, shallow-rooted cactus ripped from the earth and hurtled through the air. Manzanita bushes shook and clashed their branches until one of the smaller ones also uprooted and flew away on the tempest. The rain pounded down and always the wind increased in force.

Shrieking through the trees and howling around rock promontories, it pummeled the men and animals. It blew sheets of water in under the overhang and doused the fire. Horses whinnied in fright.

"Hurricane," Padre Miguel shouted over the incredible tumult. Another rumble sounded, this time up the canyon from them.

A foaming wall of water rushed down the creek, the trunks of small trees spun in its wake. Instantly the once placid waters rose above the banks and threatened the ledge where the men crouched out of the ferocity of the hurricane that battered the land mass of Baja California.

"We'll have to get out of here or we'll be swept away in that flash flood," Shelter yelled at the others.

Neither Raul nor Andres wanted to expose themselves. Now all manner of small trees, brush and even animals hurtled past them.

"We'll be killed," Raul protested.

"For certain if we stay here," Shelter advised. "We have to go higher up, further back."

Reluctantly the men gathered the reins of their mounts and

the two pack animals and started to struggle upward against the monumental force of the raging storm. The mighty gusts threatened to blow them off their feet and send them hurtling along to smash into canyon walls. Only grim determination kept them from fleeing in terror. Shelter rigged a rope from one man to the next, slipping it through one stirrup of each saddle. Slowly they moved on. A burro squealed wildly when a flying manzanita bush slashed into its left side. Shelter calmed the beast and peered into the murky atmosphere for some sign of protection.

Ahead he made out the darker, lumpy shapes of a cluster of boulders. He directed the desperate party that way. For long moments they crouched in the lee of the granite behemoths struggling to catch their breath. Their clothes had been soaked through, boots soggy. Even their weapons had been temporarily rendered useless. Water fell from the sky in sheets.

"Up there. See it?" Shelter shouted to the others. He pointed to a small dark spot against the nearly sheer canyon wall. "It might be a cave."

"Yes. There are caves in this canyon," Padre Miguel answered.

"We've got to get there now."

"We'll be killed if we try," Andres cried, eyes wide in fright.

The rain slackened. Slowly the wind began to diminish. A relative degree of quiet returned.

"It's the center of the storm," Padre Miguel explained. "If we hurry we can make it before the other side hits."

In a rapid scramble the four men and their animals forced their way among rocks and slippery mud to the opening of a cave. They paused there a moment and looked around them. In every direction a wall of swirling gray seemed to cut them off from the world. They could be anywhere . . . or nowhere. An eerie, shared impression made them shudder.

"Better check for snakes first," Shelter suggested.

"How? We haven't any light," Padre Miguel inquired.

They had hastily thrown their saddles over the horses' backs and from the bags attached to his, Shell produced a short stub of candle. A small metal cannister provided dry lucifer matches, one of which he struck and ignited the wick.

Shielding the tenuous flame with one hand, Shelter bent low and edged into the mouth of the cave. Shadows from the flickering light made grotesque figures on the walls. They writhed like giant serpents and hampered his efforts to make sure that no other occupants had prior claim. At last he came out.

"It's all ours."

It became necessary to hold the horses' heads low and unsaddle them to allow them to squeeze through the low opening. The last burro hardly made it to his long black tail before the hurricane struck with renewed fury.

"We're dry and safe from the wind," Shelter observed while the storm's fury lashed and howled outside.

"What about some wood for a fire?" Raul asked.

"Good idea. Take the candle and look around. Not much chance, I wouldn't think."

A yellow glow haloed Raul's head as he went further back into the cave. His cry of surprise brought them all fumbling through the dark a few minutes later.

"*Por Dios*, what is that?" the former bandit declared when the other three reached him.

Padre Miguel studied it closely. "Some sort of primitive altar, I suppose. It's made of wood."

"Do we dare disturb it?" Raul asked with superstitious dread.

"It is a pagan altar," the priest reminded him scornfully.

"Uh, yes. Yes, that's what it is." Raul stepped forward. "Who'll help me with it?"

Shelter came to the heavy slab and hefted one side. In minutes they had it split into usable lengths, about wrist thickness. The fire's warmth and brightness improved their spirits until Raul leaped to his feet, crossed himself and began

134

to mutter prayers.

"What is it, Raul?" Shelter asked.

"Look. At those. B-bones. And . . . someone has been painting things on the walls."

"Picture writing," Padre Miguel pronounced them. "Ancient savages recorded things and events here. They are harmless."

"What about the bones, Padre?"

"Sacrifices to some pagan god, Raul," the priest responded.

"There is some broken pottery here," Andres called to the others.

"I've found some, too," Morgan added. "Must be a lot of it."

"We're in some sort of religious shrine, forgotten for many centuries," Padre Miguel declared, fascination clear in the tone of his voice.

Raul felt terrified, as though sitting on another person's coffin, but summoned all his *macho* swagger to hide it.

Andres stared at the primitive artwork, unaware that it even predated his Mayan ancestors who had first visited here before Christ had been born.

"Ironic isn't it?" the Padre ruminated, "I of all people should be warming myself in the flames of an ancient artifact. Are you aware of what the church did to Mexico?" For answer he received the blank looks on the faces of his three companions. He continued. "In the culture of the Aztecs, Mayans and other Mexican Peoples, the Church perceived the handiwork of Satan. All manuscripts, observatories, even much of her architecture was destroyed, with it went the history and pride of a people. I am devoted to antiquities in the hope of making some amends." The Padre finished lamely.

Sitting with his back against the wall, Shelter Morgan felt only impatience and anxiety to get on the trail again. He burned to find El Guillo and Plaskoe's Gatling gun before another village of innocent people got massacred.

Dawn came gray and sullen to El Crucero. The hurricane

135

had passed over during the previous afternoon and a warm, tropical rain followed, nearly as heavy as that which fell during the big blow, only without the vicious winds. Two hours after sunrise, the drenching stopped. Maria Elena felt exhausted, unable to sleep during the shrieking gales and hungry from lack of anything beyond some cold beans and tortillas. After kindling a fire in the rectory kitchen stove and setting some beans to warm, she went out to look at the damage.

Naked children splashed and played in deep puddles formed by the deluge. More than a dozen houses had lost their roofs and the tile had been stripped from the belfry of the church. More hard work for people already driven almost to the limit. All around her she saw defeat in sad, lax faces.

"Come on, you people. We can't let this stop us. Clear out the rubble. Start fixing your roofs. Do you want to get caught by the next rain?"

"It is the end of the world," an old crone told her. "What would you, an outsider, know about what is good for El Crucero. God wants this town to die."

"No! That is not true. Wait until Padre Miguel returns. He'll tell you. For now we have to build, clean up. Make the best of our lot. It is the only way."

A feeble voice cried from under a pile of collapsed adobe and timbers.

"There's someone trapped in there. Don't just stand around," Maria Elena berated some of the men. "Get shovels. Dig them out."

Slowly, like figures in a dream, the men turned to the task. Maria Elena chaffed at their laggardly efforts and snatched a shovel from one villager's hand. She began to fling mud and adobe chunks to both sides of her.

At last the rescuers broke through. A pale hand and frightened face could be seen in a small pocket created by a countertop and the vigas of a ribbed ceiling that had fallen in on it. The hole enlarged quickly and the freed woman pulled to safety. A small boy standing near by, who was not yet aware he had been orphaned in the raid, looked up and his face bloomed with happiness.

"Papi," he shouted and began to run toward the far end of the street before anyone could hold him back.

The naked boy, dripping red-brown water from the pool he had been playing in, ran gleefully toward a man sitting on his light brown horse. In his mind, the youngster saw it as his father returning. Maria Elena looked after him and her blood chilled in sudden horror.

"Come back!" she screamed. "Pablo, come back!"

Too late her warning reached his ears. The child ran, gurgling with joy, to the side of the snorting horse. The happy seven-year-old got a .45 slug between his eyes for his efforts.

Maria Elena's shriek of terror was drowned out by maniacal laughter.

El Guillo and his bandits had come back.

15.

Experience over the long months and years of his search had taught Shelter Morgan to be prepared for nearly anything. Consequently he had along in his saddle bags some emergency rations. Dried peas, beans and some jerked beef, a hard cone of sticky brown sugar and a small square of salt. He had even managed to stash a quarter pound of coffee beans in a little burlap sack. Once the fire blazed cheerily, he set about preparing the meal they lost to the hurricane.

In the soft sand of the cave floor, Padre Miguel found a nearly complete olla. This they set out in the deluge to wash and test for leaks. It met the requirements, at least for Shelter and the priest. Raul Sanchez didn't seem quite so enthused.

"You mean we eat out of the bowls of the dead?" he asked incredulously.

"Why not?" Morgan returned. "They won't complain."

"H-how do you know that . . . for sure, I mean."

"Raul, the dead are dead. Their spirits have gone," he added with a diffident look at Padre Miguel, "to wherever they deserved to go. The former owners of these implements are not hanging around here to haunt us or get revenge. They no longer have anything to do with earthly things."

"He is right, Raul," the priest took up. "Widows and children eat from pots provided by dead men. No harm comes to them. Or the items are sold through a used dealer and others have them without fear."

"I . . . very well, if you say so, Padre," Raul surrendered reluctantly.

Although not a feast, the meal filled empty bellies and warmed chilled bodies. Padre Miguel found a stone mortar and pestle, with which Morgan ground the coffee beans and another olla provided a pot to make the brew. The most violent cell of the hurricane passed beyond them, after stalling for a long time on the high peaks around the canyon. Throughout the night, though, a torrential, tropical downpour continued. The falling water felt warm and, after the wind declined, Shelter stripped, took a bar of yellowed lye soap from his saddle bags and stepped out into it for a bath. A few moments later, Andres joined him.

"You have many scars, *Señor* Morgan," the young man observed.

"Eh?" Shelter didn't recognize the word.

Hesitantly, like a shy child, Andres reached out and circled a puckered bullet hole scar in Shell's left shoulder. *"Cicatriz,"* he repeated. *"Marcas de combate."*

"Oh . . . Yep. That one is very old," Shell said slowly in his limited Spanish. "One of the men I seek gave it to me."

"The *gringo* named Plaskoe?"

"No, but one much like him." Morgan turned his back to let the cascading downpour wash the soap from his chest and spoke over his shoulder. "They stole some gold from my men and I. Gold that belonged to the Confederate Army."

"Ah. That is bad. And they tried to kill all of you?"

"They succeeded, except for me. Now I hunt them."

"To put them in jail, no?"

"To kill every last one of them."

Andres wisely said nothing more. Morgan finished, handed the youth the soap and went back inside to dry off by the fire.

A dull, gray morning found the storm nearly gone. The rain had slackened to a light mist with occasional heavier showers. Slipping and sliding, the four men negotiated the slope and discovered that little had been lost to the hurricane. One pack-saddle had been smashed against a tree and the granite coffee pot had disappeared entirely, along with all the lighter cooking

139

utensils and the tucker box. Shelter shrugged philosophically. They could reoutfit in El Crucero.

"There's no hope of following the trail now," he told the others of his decision. "We'll go back to El Crucero, tell the men what we learned and what we accomplished, four against forty, and perhaps plan some sort of ambush for them when they try to reach that hideout Maria Elena described to us."

El Guillo stood in the plaza of El Crucero with a happy smile on his lips. He rested his hands on his spreading hips and looked Maria Elena up and down with immense satisfaction. He clutched a coiled bullwhip.

"You thought you could escape El Guillo?" he asked the girl.

"Yes, you filthy pig. I thought I was well away from the sight of you."

"How was it I missed you the first time?"

"I hid."

"And my men did not find you? That is strange." He stepped close to her, transferred the whip from right to left hand. Then he swung hard, leaving a palm print on her left cheek. "You are, and always will be, my woman. You are like no other woman since my . . . my dear wife. You are young and healthy and can keep my *verga* stiff and content. Also, I have a small boy. My son needs a mother. You can be there with him when I am gone. There won't be many more raids. Then you will share my future good fortune."

"Ha!" Maria Elena cried defiantly. "Bandidos never quit until the Federales hang them or shoot them down like the dogs they are."

El Guillo slapped her again. It staggered the girl and she shrank back. If only her dear Shelter was here, she thought in desperation. El Guillo took her roughly by one elbow and began to steer her toward a small two room adobe dwelling set back from the plaza.

140

"Miguel!" The bandit leader shouted, then gave his instructions. "You see this woman? If she escapes again it will be your *cajones*, take whatever men you need and maintain a guard on her at all times. You will see she is treated with all proper respect as my wife. Do you understand?"

"*Si Jefe.*"

"That . . . uh, what you did the night you escaped from the *cala*. I'm interested to see if you can put me to sleep again. We're going in here and you'll give it a try, no?"

"And if I don't?"

"Oh, you will, *chiquita*. You will."

"I'll bite it off."

"Being slapped twice is not enough? Do you want a taste of my whip? But that will not be necessary. I want you to think of my son. He is seven years old and so lonely for a mother. He is a good boy, a bit wild, I suppose. He has the face of an angel. Think of him. You would not make some, ah, sacrifice for the sake of a child?"

El Guillo sounded almost pleading, hardly himself, Maria Elena thought as they entered the small house. In the bedroom, El Guillo unfastened and lowered his trousers, exposing his swollen manhood. Then he seated himself on the sagging mattress of an ancient brass bed.

"Now. Let us see, shall we?"

Quickly, quite business-like, Maria Elena serviced him through two unceasing climaxes. Then she paused and smiled coquettishly at him. "You really don't want me to put you to sleep, do you?"

"Ummm. Perhaps not. That . . . that method takes a lot out of a man, did you know that?"

"Oh, yes. Long ago, when I was little, a friend of mine and I used that way to take the swagger out of a young *caballero*. His father, the *haciendado*, could not understand why his son ached for three days afterward."

To her surprise, El Guillo slapped his bare thigh and laughed uproariously. "That is a good story, *chica*. You have fire, spirit.

141

I like that and so will my son."

"Tell me," Maria Elena pondered aloud while she raised herself and sat beside the bandit leader, one hand caressing his chest. "What did you mean about only another raid or two?"

"I have had a dream for many years. I wish to be respectable. To lead the life of a *haciendado*. What? You seem surprised. What is wrong with that? The life of a bandit is not what I want for my son. I want to live on the land, to work it and make it pay for me. I want my son to grow up being respected by those around us. To do that takes much money.

"I will make one more big raid. If that is not enough, I have a grand plan that will insure it."

"What is that?"

"Have you ever heard of El Triumpho?"

"No."

"There is much gold and silver there. More than in all the rest of Baja California. Twice a year plate ships take it away to the mainland. Before that time comes again, I can sail my men down to La Paz, ride inland and steal that horde of gold. My share will more than buy me a rancho in Sonora or Guanajuato. And so I become a man of stature, of substance and respect."

"You are a strange man, El Guillo."

"Please. Call me Rudolfo."

Maria Elena wanted to giggle. Rudolfo the Terror of Baja. No wonder he took the name El Guillo. *The Leader* sounded a lot more *macho* than Rudolfo. El Guillo spoke again.

"*Tengo un gusano de la conciencia*, I have great remorse," he repeated, "about how I have raised my son since his mother died. Understand me, please, I want him to have a mother. You have all the qualities I would desire."

"Is . . . is this a proposal of marriage?"

"No," El Guillo snapped, suddenly himself again. "It is a demand."

Later that night, while a sated El Guillo snored on the sagging bed, Maria Elena rose and slipped barefoot into the kitchen. Her mind seethed in turmoil. Images of the butchered men, women and children of her own village of La Rumorosa and those of El Crucero mingled with the sight of a suddenly tender and touchingly vulnerable Rudolfo Santacruz, talking about his hopes for his son. El Guillo indeed. Guided by a desire for revenge, though pulled by a burgeoning of maternal instinct, she silently searched the shelves for the object she wanted most. At last she found it. A long, keenly sharp knife. Clutching it to her breast, she returned to the bedroom.

Maria Elena took a deep breath, gripped the handle of the butcher knife tightly and raised it above her head. Did she really want to strike? a portion of her mind taunted her. She hesitated and fought to stifle a gasp of internal conflict.

Lightning fast, El Guillo came awake. His arm lashed out and strong brown fingers closed around Maria Elena's wrist. Arrested in mid-plunge, the knife gleamed in the moonlight entering through a window.

"So. This is how you would reward me for my revelation?"

Naked, El Guillo climbed from the bed, plucked the knife from Maria Elena's hand and reached for his whip.

"Have there always been bandits like El Guillo in Mexico?" Shelter asked Padre Miguel as they rode along the muddy road to El Crucero.

"Oh, yes, of course. It is a way of life for many in a land too rich in people and too poor in work. Before the bandits, we had pirates."

"Pirates?"

"Certainly. Two of the most famous were English. The biggest haul was made by the buccaneer Tom Cavendish, who took the largest prize ever. He captured the Manilla galleon, *Santa Ana*, as she approached the tip of Baja, near Cabo San Lucas on November the Fourth, Fifteen Eighty-seven. He escaped with many millions in dubloons and pieces of eight. It bought him a knighthood."

"Who was the other one?"

143

"Ah! You do not know? He became quite famous for another reason entirely. Once a privateer, commissioned by the English King to raid Spanish commerce in the New World, Oliver Cromwell came to the Sea of Cortez. One of the small coves near the bay at La Paz is where his crews careened his three ships. It is named for him to this day, *La Playa Coromuel*, Cromwell Beach. He lay there for weeks after making the repairs. Then they sailed to attack the plate ships taking gold and silver from the mines at El Triumpho to the mainland. Then he shaped course home to Britain. There he used his money to organize a heretic religion, it was called, I think, the Round Heads, or the Know Nothing Church. Cromwell preached that ignorance was the state desired for man by God. The less a man knew, the closer to Holiness he came. To know nothing, you see? He also taught sedition and rebellion. At last, he fomented an uprising against the king, ousted and murdered him and ruled England for a number of years.

"Eventually young Prince Charles defeated Cromwell's forces and many were exiled to Europe. There they followed their same principals of subversion and sedition and got thrown out of every host country they descended upon. Later, under a new name . . . Puritans, I think it was, they came to your country and settled in a place called Plymouth Rock in Massachusetts."

"Like I told you before, Padre, I never got much formal schooling. But it seems to me that this Cromwell never forgot his piratical ways."

Padre Miguel laughed warmly. "You have an incisive mind, Sheltor. No one since Cromwell's time has ever successfully stolen the produce of the smelters at El Triumpho."

"Why is that?"

Padre Miguel waved a hand to encompass the land south of them. "That is all desert down there. From here to the tip of the peninsula. It is over seven hundred miles from Bahia de Los Angeles to La Paz. Seventeen more to El Triumpho. The logistics of a land expedition would make such an attempt impossible. Without powerful warships the plate shipments could never be taken again. The Mexican Navy patrols the sea lanes between Baja and the mainland."

"Considering El Guillo's taste for gold, I wouldn't put it past him to think of such a raid."

Conversation ended as they increased their speed. El Crucero lay another day's ride ahead.

Mud. Everywhere mud. Tom Plaskoe cursed the gluey substance that clung to the wheels of his carreta. Loaded with spoils he was taking to the gang's special cache, as well as the heavy Gatling gun, the boxy cart mired down at the least opportunity. Stuck again, Plaskoe fumed when his best efforts with whip, voice and straining muscles would not free the left side wheel. He reached up to the driver's seat and took a machete with him to cut brush to shove under the mud-imprisoned wheel.

Half an hour of sweaty labor brought him no relief. The sound of hoofs clopping through the mire brought his attention around to the direction in which he headed. A tall, smiling Mexican, riding a fine horse approached. The stranger touched the brim of his big sombrero and greeted Plaskoe politely.

"It's not such a good day," Plaskoe answered testily, "when you're stuck in the mud."

"Perhaps I can be of assistance, *Señor*."

"I could sure use it. And I appreciate it, believe me."

The well-dressed man turned in his saddle and waved a hand. "Arturo, Pepe, Antonio, come forward. This gentleman needs help."

Six men answered his summons. In silence, with straining muscles, they easily extricated the carreta from its deep pit of sludge. Thank goodness he had only five miles to go, Plaskoe thought. A small wriggle of discomfort nagged at his mind. There seemed to be some elusive quality about these men, an

145

invisible aura of wrongness. Slowly Plaskoe eased himself to the back of the cart. He felt relieved that he always traveled on these missions prepared for any eventuality. With a grunt he swung up into the wagon box and began to undo the lacings of a large canvas cover.

"Want to make sure everything is all right. Took quite a jolt when I hit that mudhole."

"It is good that you check, Señor. We would be most unhappy if anything had been damaged. A man well dressed as you are, with so large a carreta, we could only speculate that your cargo must be of great value."

"Not really," Plaskoe dismissed as he continued to loosen tie-ropes.

"Oh, come now, Señor. We are men of the world, no? My friends and I, we are also shrewd judges of a man's worth." The stranger reached to his waistband and a cocked Colt appeared in his hand.

"If you please, Señor. Show us this most valuable cargo."

"It's really not what you think," Plaskoe stalled.

"Be quick, Señor, or we will kill you first and check what we have taken later."

"If you insist," Plaskoe relented.

With one hand he pulled away the tarpaulin while the other grabbed under it and secured the crank. When the canvas came free, he began to turn. With the training mechanism disengaged, he could aim the mighty weapon with one hand while he fired it with the other.

One inch slugs from the Gatling gun turned two of the bandits into huge sprays of pulped flesh and shattered bone. Their leader got off one wild shot with his Colt that cracked past Plaskoe's ear. Instantly, Plaskoe swung the revolving barrel system in that direction.

Battered by the tremendous muzzle blasts, even the trained war horses of the bandidos revolted, their pitching denying return fire.

Two more of the outlaws died screaming, their chests turned

into hollow pits of gore. Realization came too late to the leader in the second before he looked down the six rotating muzzles.

"You are the *gringo* who rides with El Guillo!" he cried as the one inch slugs spit from the Gatling toward his vulnerable hide.

"Must not have been your day, feller," Plaskoe observed dryly while he splashed the bandit and his remaining two men into sodden mounds of ruined flesh.

16.

El Cruceros' skyline was poorer by three more ravaged buildings when Shelter Morgan and his companions returned from their search. One of those destroyed had been the church. Revenge, they knew without speaking of it, for Padre Miguel taking part in the attack on the bandits at Mission Santa Maria. Sobbing women and frightened children ran out to greet them.

"Maria Elena?" Shelter asked first. "Where is she?"

"Taken away by El Guillo," fat Guadalupe wailed, chubby hands pressed to her tear-stained cheeks.

"Damn!"

A youngster in his early teens stepped forward, straw sombrero clutched respectfully in both hands before his chest. "S-she was . . . was savagely beaten with a whip by El Guillo. She tried to kill him with a knife it is said."

"That bastard," Shelter growled. "We'll get supplies and head out after them at once." He stood in his stirrups, looking over the crowd for the men. He spotted only five. "We have fought the bandits once. There aren't so many of them now. Will you men come with us?"

Silence followed.

"Where would we go to catch El Guillo by surprise?" Raul asked for those there.

"To the place Maria Elena told me about. To Bahia de Los Angeles."

The five men talked animatedly among themselves. At last three reluctantly stepped forward.

"We will go with you, *Señor* Morgan."

"Good. Get your animals ready, food and supplies. Arm yourselves well. We will leave in half an hour."

"If we are to ride around Parador without being seen, this is the trail to take, *Jefe*," Juan Rubio reminded his leader.

"Who says we are going to ride around Parador, Juan?"

"You mean . . . ?"

"*Si*. Exactly," El Guillo told his lieutenant. "For too long we have let Parador escape our attentions. They will have grown soft, fat, overconfident . . . and rich. It is time to relieve them of some of those riches, no? Also we can show that *gringo* that we do not need him and his magic gun in order to raid a town. *Andele, muchachos!*"

Pablo Ordonez liked being *alcalde* of Parador. Think of it, he often told his wife, mayor of a large village at the age of only thirty-five. Who knows where it might lead? Governor of the state? *Presidente* of Mexico?

Sarafina, his patient spouse, thought his political ambitions to be foolish. At least here, in Parador, he was a big *gusano* in a small maguay. Away from this country village, what would he be? Still a worm, only now a small one to be stepped on by the clever men who lived in big cities. Better to stay where they belonged.

Not so, Pablo would contend. He was ready for bigger things. He was not ready, though, to fight off bandits. He came running from his office in shirt-sleeves when the clamor began.

The church bell rang loudly and a young man who worked for Martinez at the dairy came running down the street shouting at the top of his voice.

"*Bandidos! Bandidos!* They are coming into town from the north. Everyone hide. Run for your lives!"

"No," the mayor said calmly. Then he raised his voice.

"Don't hide! Don't run away. Get your guns and we will fight them." He grabbed the excited young Victor by one arm. "How many of them are there?"

"Maybe thirty. They had big *pistolas* and many rifles. They are shooting everyone."

"Quick, then. Run through the town. Tell the men and older boys to bring their guns to the square."

Decisively, Pablo went around the square ordering carts and wagons to be dragged into place to block all of the streets. "Women and children to the church," he called out over and over. He looked down the street and saw that the bandits had been halted by unexpected resistance from the grist mill. That would give him time.

"*Dios!* How many of them are there?" Juan Rubio asked his leader.

"I don't know, Juan," El Guillo admitted to his lieutenant. "More than should be. They should have been blasted out of there, running like frightened chickens."

"*Si*," Juan agreed. "That is how it has always been over the past four years. If . . ." he went on against his own prejudices, "the *gringo* was here it would this time."

"*Mierda!* Shit!" El Guillo repeated angrily. "We can take a little village without his help. Rally the men and send some around to the other side. We will take this small mill, eh?"

Emilio Montez took careful aim with his ancient shotgun and blasted a running bandit off his feet. Attack his mill would they. What did they want? Feed for their horses? They could pay for it like anyone else, the mill owner fumed. He reloaded and turned at the sound of scraping boots in the hopper room behind him.

Juan Rubio stepped through the door, clothes whitened from flour. "*Adios, molinero*," he gloated. Juan had counted the shots and knew the miller had emptied his double gun.

Emilio Montez struck a deadly blow to El Guillo's gang when

150

his charge of buckshot disintegrated Juan's sternum and sprayed the miller's office with bits of shirt, bone and flesh.

"They're coming!" a clerk from the bank yelled.

Mayor Ordonez tightened his grip around the small of the stock of his 11mm Spanish Remington. He knew that the three hundred seventy-five grain bullet, pushed by seventy-eight grains of black powder, could knock even that big fat bandido in the center of the charging outlaws from his saddle. Quickly he checked his hastily constructed defenses.

The door to the church had been closed and tightly barred. Tables and empty barrels from the cantina, hurriedly filled with sand, had been added to the barricades, giving some feeling of security. More than sixty men and some twenty boys, fourteen or over, crowded behind the accumulation of wagons, mattresses and barrels. Many had become pale white and their lips moved in mumbled prayers, curses or self-argument. Yet none made a move to leave. Good. This could hardly be the feared El Guillo, Pablo decided. Where was the powerful gun that leveled barricades and turned buildings into powder? Only a block separated the defenders from the onrushing mauraders.

Ordonez brought the big rolling-block rifle to his shoulder and took aim. The bandits fired to both sides as they raced toward the obstruction. Firmly the mayor squeezed the trigger of the Spanish Remington.

It went off with a shoulder-jarring thump.

Fifteen hundred and ninety pounds of muzzle energy smashed into the bandit next to the leader and drove him out of the saddle. The 375 grain slug turned one lung to jelly and snapped his spine, so that the bandido twitched and flopped like a demented puppet as he lay in the street. To both sides of the mayor, more of the townsmen opened up.

*　　　*　　　*

"Turn off! Turn off . . . down that alley," El Guillo yelled over the din of exploding arms.

The column of bandits swung to the left and raced into the safety of a narrow *callejon* between two adobe buildings. Too late the leader discovered his mistake. The alley had also been barricaded. Half way down, his men came under fire from ahead and from windows and rooftops on both sides.

A bandit screamed and fell from his horse, to be ground into raspberry mush by the churning hoofs of his companions' mounts. Another moaned and slumped over his animal's mane and clung to it as the gang milled in confusion a long while before racing for the street again.

"They'll be waiting for us out there," one gap-toothed outlaw confided to another.

"That is true. At least there we have a chance to shoot back."

Behind them, El Guillo bellowed commands to hurry, to look out for the defenders in the square and to act like men. His own heart pounded furiously and he sweat profusely. He could not remember a time he had been so afraid in an attack. It was that damned gun. That cursed *gringo's* Gatling gun. It had made mice of them all. He saw a white face appear in the second floor window of a building across from the alley and threw a rapid shot.

Blood splashed from the sharpshooter's head on the broken glass in the remaining pane and he fell away. That made El Guillo feel considerably better. He broke into the clear and spurred his horse, not toward the plaza, but back the way they had come.

"Follow me! Back to the edge of town. We have to think this over, be wise in what we do," he shouted. Handicapped by the loss of his best lieutenant, he felt compelled to explain everything in detail to his men.

They streamed along behind him, firing over their shoulders at the staunch villagers, who shouted imprecations at them and kept up a steady shower of lead.

They had beaten them off, Pablo Ordonez rejoiced. He knew only too well, though, that the bandits would be back. "Load your weapons, men. Keep shells at hand. They will come back."

"Three men have been killed, *Señor Alcalde*," a swamper from the cantina reported. "Two wounded. *Señora* Montenegro has taken them into the cantina to be cared for.

"Lucky devils," a *vaquero* from a local ranch remarked. "I could use a little care from the cantina."

"Have Ignacio roll out a barrel of *cerveza* for our thirst," the mayor commanded. "The village treasury will pay for it."

The swamper hurried off to do as he had been bid.

"Wet your throats with beer, men and get ready for them to come back."

"What can we do?" one bandit asked his leader. Blood ran from a bullet graze along the side of the man's left arm.

"To be honest, I don't know. We should never have stopped to fight it out at that mill. That gave too much time for the village fools to make ready. We will need a clever plan." El Guillo brooded over it in silence for a long five minutes. At last he brightened.

"We will have to burn them out. Set fires all around the plaza and drive them into the open. They have trapped themselves, not us."

"If we burn the town down, what can we get for loot?"

El Guillo scowled. "You are right, Francisco. No, we cannot burn them out. I tell you, this is an awful situation. If only we had the Gatling gun."

"I thought," a bandit El Guillo did not see said sarcastically, "that we were going to show everyone that we didn't need the

153

gringo and his Gatling gun."

"Who said that?" El Guillo growled. The flames of his anger died quickly. They had gotten into a bad situation. He had lost too many men already. The men of Parador had too many guns and much ammunition. It could turn into a slaughter for his men. What to do?

"If we can't burn them out, how do we go about it?" Francisco inquired.

"Let me think, damnit!"

"They are coming from this way now," a stooped, myopic tailor called out from his place on the defenses.

"This way, too," a squeaky-voiced boy of fourteen added from his perch in a tree.

"I see some down the street over here," a third voice added.

"They are on foot and they have torches with them."

"Don't let them burn the town!" the banker wailed, aware that his establishment had notes on nearly every business and dwelling in Parador. If they burned to the ground he would be wiped out.

"Hold fire until they get in close. We want to see what they intend to do," Mayor Ordonez ordered.

The bandits came closer. Then their strategy became clear. They would not burn the town down around the defenders, they would fill the plaza with blazing brands and burn the defenders out from behind their barricades. Blazing flambeaux flew through the air to land among the boxes, barrels and wooden furniture that made up the barricade. Others fell among the grim men standing in defense of their village. A few cartwheeled deeper into the plaza, trailing sparks, to strike in the branches of trees or extinguish themselves when they struck the hard ground.

"Open fire!" the mayor commanded.

A hail of zipping, cracking bullets laced through the air of each street that gave onto the plaza. Bandits howled and groaned and fell in heaps. Others returned fire, while scrambling away to the security of their horses.

"We haven't any choice," El Guillo told his surviving men. "They are too strong for us. We have grown too dependent on Tomas and his Gatling gun. Nine men dead, eleven seriously wounded. All this for a ridiculous nine hundred pesos in the miller's office drawer. Too big a price is what I say. Round the men up and we go. Head for the trail to Bahia de Los Angeles. We need rest and a chance to reorganize."

17.

Bullet holes pockmarked many buildings along the main street of Parador when Shelter Morgan and his small band of five arrived there. It presented an all too familiar pattern. Yet startling differences became immediately apparent.

Unlike the doleful villages that had been ravaged by El Guillo and his desperados, Parador seemed in a festive mood. Bright desert sunlight made everything a dazzle and the crystal air hung heavy with the succulent odors of roasting meat, corn, chili peppers and onions. Two trumpets hung brilliant shards of sound on the breeze, accompanied by a band playing the ooompah and thump of spirited *paso dobles*, and from the barricaded plaza ahead came an almost sensual chant.

"*O-le! . . . O--le! . . . Oo---le!*" Crackling applause rippled around the square.

"What the hell?" Shelter Morgan blurted. "You'd think El Guillo hadn't been here."

"Oh, he has," Padre Miguel advised. "Only it seems things didn't go his way. We've arrived in time for a *festival.*"

"These people got their town shot up and they're celebrating?"

"The significant thing is that the village was attacked . . . but the bandidos did not win. They must have been preparing for some sort of festivities, or they could never have had enough men in town to stand them off. Neither would they have had the animals on hand, or any *matadores* available to fight."

Shelter looked blank. Raul saw his confusion and added his

156

own bit of enlightenment.

"*La Fiesta Brava*. The, what is it the Yanquis say? Ah, the boolfights. It is customary in these larger villages to have a *corrida*, perhaps two matadors and four bools, at their religious or national fiestas. Because there are no *ganadarias* in Baja California, the *torros* must be shipped here from the mainland. That takes time. The same for *Matadores de Torros*. The killers of bools. This must have been the day for the *fiesta*, so people had been coming into town for some time. They would have easily outnumbered El Guillo's men. So now they have double the cause to have a *fiesta*."

The six men halted their horses at a crowded tie-rail half a block from the central square of Parador and walked to the barrier that cordoned off the hard dirt of the plaza. Spectators gave them hard and suspicious looks at first until they saw Padre Miguel's brown Franciscan robe. Word of the new arrivals spread rapidly through the audience. In the sandy arena formed by the barricade, a team of skitterish mules, hitched to a single-tree pattered their tiny hoofs and strained into the burden of a large, black, very dead bull that lay on the sand in a pool of its own blood. A lone trumpeter, seated on a balcony with four other people, rose and placed his instrument to his lips. A sign from an expensively dressed man with a light tan *cordobesa* stopped him. The official dressed in the cordoban suit and hat rose and addressed himself to the new arrivals.

"I have been informed that we have some visitors at our *festival*. I am *Don* Pablo Ordonez, *alcalde* of Parador. If you come in peace, you are welcome."

"I am Padre Miguel Espinoza, rector of the church at El Crucero, where these four men come from also." The priest named the visitors, then introduced El Tiburon and Shelter Morgan. "This is Raul Manuel Sanchez y Hertado, a brave man from the State of Chihuahua, formerly of the Fourth Lancers regiment. And this *Norteño* is *Capitan* Shelter Morgan of the Confederate States of America. Be assured we come in peace, *Don* Pablo, as far as Parador is concerned. Our business is with

157

a bandido who calls himself El Guillo. We seek to hunt him out and kill him and all who ride with him."

A cheer went up from the crowd.

"Take me along!" a voice cried.

"Take me also," another man called.

"We have beaten him once. Let us finish it," yet another young man declared.

"Amazing what a little victory will do," Shelter observed dryly.

"Then you are most welcome here. And, Padre, I believe I have a surprise for you. Do you, by chance, have a brother named Fernando Espinosa? A *matador de torros*?"

"I do."

"Then rejoice. He is on the *cartel* for this *festival*. After the *corrida*, we will feast and you may be reunited with your brother."

"Thank you."

The trumpeter blew the haunting notes of the *clarin* and another ferocious bull thundered into the improvised ring. This one had mottled white-and-black hindquarters and a gray-white underbelly. He charged straight and true, snorting and shaking his head, long strings of saliva flying from his frothing mouth. His inborn fury had been heightened by long confinement and the pin-prick bite of the *devisa*, the barbed stick holding the colored ribbons and burgonette of the breeding ranch from which he came, in his shoulder.

Shelter did not understand what it was he watched, though he looked on with avid fascination.

A slender young man in a brightly colored, tight-fitting costume stepped from behind a small target-like barrier and unfurled a large magenta and yellow cape. Sunlight sparkled from the gold thread and sequins that decorated his short jacket and the broad stripe down his trouser legs. He stepped forward and called to the raging animal, further attracting its attention with a flick of one corner of the *capote*.

The huge beast set itself, then launched a charge that

brought it rapidly across two thirds of the square, The cape belled before it, then turned concave, engulfing the mighty head and fearsome horns as it swung in a smooth circle around the young matador's legs.

"Ole!" the crowd cheered.

"This *lance* is called a *Veronica*," Padre Miguel explained. "Watch, he will do three or so, then end with one of several terminating *lances*, a *farol*, which raises the *capote* up over his head and into position behind him, or a *rebolera*, where he swings the cape in a swirl around his waist, most likely."

So it went. After two series, accompanied by cheers, a man on horseback, both heavily armored, entered the arena. He carried a long, metal-tipped lance. At the matador's discretion, he placed his spear in the bull's shoulder twice, boring deeply on the left side. Padre Miguel explained that this was done to correct a bad tendency of the bull to hook with his horns. Such a trait could prove rapidly fatal to the matador. Satisfied with the punishment, the matador graciously gave the second *quite*, or take-away to his colleague. Then they both retired to the barrier.

Two young men entered the ring, each armed only with colorfully decorated sticks that ended in hooked barbs of hand-forged iron. One at a time, they cited the bull with nothing but their vulnerable bodies.

"The *bandarilleros* will place the sticks according to their matador's instructions," Padre Miguel instructed Shelter. "The *bandarillas* are far more important than mere decoration. They help insure the animal will charge and move his horns in the desired manner. They don't hurt so much as irritate."

"It's all sort of bloody," Shelter observed, not at all so sure he appreciated what he saw.

"It is an ancient ritual, a drama of life and death. It is not a sport. Don't be deceived by that thought. There is nothing fair about it, as is the case with sports. It is certain, foreordained if you will, that one or the other will die. The bull . . . or the man. Sometimes it is both."

"I'm curious. As a priest, how do you see this?"

Taken off guard by the question, Padre Miguel thought for a moment while the last pair of bandarillas, making a total of six, was placed. "As an arm of the church, I must condemn the unnecessary risking of human life. As a man, one whose ancestory is steeped in centuries of the *fiesta*, I must say it touches me, excites me and draws my admiration. Raw courage and the mind of man against brute force, so quick, so ferocious that few dare to stand against them. But I am making a sermon of this. Let us watch and enjoy."

The matador had returned to the arena. This time he bore a small, red cape, supported on its upper side by a stick. It was folded into a narrow triangle and across it his thumb secured the slender blade of a sword. He stopped under the mayor's balcony and removed the small, ornately embroidered black hat he wore and raised it and the cape to the official. Requesting permission to kill the bull, Padre Miguel explained.

A solemn nod signified approval. Then the matador walked half way around the plaza to where Shelter Morgan sat with Padre Miguel and their small group. The slim, graceful young man raised his hat, a *montera*, the priest called it, once more, this time pointed at Padre Miguel. He spoke in rapid Spanish, kissed his *montera*, turned about and tossed it over his head into Padre Miguel's lap. Enormous applause rose from the crowd.

"What was all that about?" Shelter asked.

"He dedicated the bull to me."

"That's an honor?" Shelter shrugged. "I suppose it is, all considered. What did he say?"

Padre Miguel cast his gaze downward and flushed slightly. "He said, 'I dedicate this bull to my brother, a man of God with the courage of the bravest bull ever born.'"

"*That's* your brother?"

"Yes."

"I don't know much about this, but I think he does a terrific job."

"He does. Some day he will be the greatest matador in Mexico."

"If he lives that long," Shelter added.

"You're learning, my son. Now, watch his *faína*."

The subtleties escaped Shelter Morgan in a montage of *passas por alta*, *derichasos*, *mulinados*, *pendulos* and the *muleta* version of the *farol*. They were only names, connected to graceful and dangerous-looking swirls of the red cloth. At last, Fernando Espinosa went to the sidelines and exchanged his work sword for the sharp-edged killing instrument. A short series of passes and he lined the bull up.

His sword came from hiding behind the cloth. He placed his hand, holding the wooden-pommeled hilt, to his cheek, sighting down the slim, curved blade. He poised himself on the ball of his left foot, right leg raised slightly, toes on the ground, heel against his left shin. The red cape hung downward in his left hand, the skirt on the ground only a scant three feet from the nose of the bedazzled bull.

The mighty head moved slowly from side to side, uncertain. "This is the most dangerous moment," Padre Miguel told Shelter.

"After all that has gone on?"

"Oh, yes. The bull is tired, but he is still faster and more dangerous than the man. Watch."

Fernando flicked the edge of his cape. The bull charged.

With one step forward, Fernando thrust and buried the sword to the hilt behind the huge head as he drew the animal's charge across his body and under his extended sword arm.

A bellow of real pain came from the dying bull. It took two tottering steps and fell on its side. The spectators went wild.

Hats flew into the ring, shoes, goat-skin bags of wine and a lady's shawl. A sea of white cloths surged above the heads of cheering men and women. The band played in a frenzy.

"Watch the *authoridad*," Padre Miguel suggested to Shelter as he pointed to the mayor.

From an inside pocket of his jacket, Mayor Ordonez produced a handkerchief, which he raised once . . . then again. A man dressed in a charro costume stepped out and cut both ears from the dead bull. These he raised to the balcony, turned and gave them to the matador, accompanied by a back-slapping *abrasso*.

"Two ears. That's not bad at all. Let's go around to the building where the mayor is sitting. I want you to meet my brother," Padre Miguel suggested.

The party went on for three hours. Although sundown neared, Shelter wanted to press on. His small posse had been increased by fifteen volunteers from Parador. Heavily armed, with supplies and sturdy mounts, they gathered at the edge of town. After making good-byes and thanks to the mayor and Matador Fernando Espinoza, Shelter, Padre Miguel and Raul joined them.

"According to Andres, the trail leads southeast, toward Bahia de Los Angeles," Shelter told his expedition. "From what Maria Elena said, they will be right where we want them. We'll ride until dark, camp, then move on at first light."

Bahia de Los Angeles! Whoever named it, Shelter Morgan thought, had a strange idea of what angels would like. With the exception of parts of Nevada and Utah, Shelter had never seen such desolate, forbidding terrain.

The sparkling, salt waters of the Gulf of California, called the Sea of Cortez by the Mexicans, could not offer relief from the arid, rock-strewn countryside. Fresh water came at a premium, a commodity nearly as precious as gold. After leaving Parador, they encountered nothing that could be called a village. Here and there a cluster of drab houses, a small building that held a combination grocery and *pulqueria*, an occasional cantina and inn. The land could support few, the water supply even less. The twenty-one man force rode down off the escarpment onto the flat tidal plains an hour past mid-day, two days after leaving Parador. They had seen no sign of the bandits.

"What now?" Raul inquired.

"We ask around. There are boats on the water. Fishermen, no doubt. That means they will have homes, families. Someone should know about a force the size of El Guillo's," Shelter surmised.

Shelter, Raul and Padre Miguel in the lead, they trotted on until the detachment came to a cluster of dwellings close by the water. Deep grooves in the sand marked the passage of boat keels and the smell of drying fish, decaying entrails and salt left no doubt as to the purpose of this rude hamlet.

"Good afternoon," Shelter greeted a wizened old man packing stiff, flat whole fish into barrels layered with salt. "We re looking for some friends."

"No one comes to Bahia de Los Angeles, *Señor*," the old man replied. "Who is it you seek? Roberto Castro, who has a large family and all fish here? Or is it Paco Nuñez, who has eleven brothers? Them I know."

"These men might be strangers," Shelter went on through Padre Miguel's translation. "Who have come here only recently. Maybe one or two times before?"

The elderly fisherman paused to scratch his thinning white hair with a blackened, cracked fingernail. "I know of no such people, *Señor*."

At three other fishing camps they received the same sort of information. No one seemed to know of a large number of men, bandits or not. They continued southward down the shore of the bay, looking out at Isla La Guarda and wondering.

Maria Elena had said something about a land-locked cove. Shelter tried asking about that.

"There are many such, *Señor*. This is rough country. With more than thirty-five miles of bayshore, coves like you speak of are common. Then there is the big island. No one lives there and there are no roads at all. Therefore nearly any inlet would be land-locked from behind the beach."

No help at all. With a fatalistic shrug, the ex-Confederate led his mixed band further south. Evening found them five mile distant from the last fishing camp they visited.

"How could we have missed them on the road if they haven' reached here yet?" Shelter asked aloud.

"Another trail, perhaps?" Raul suggested.

"That is a definite possibility," Padre Miguel speculated "Maria said they left their horses behind with fishermen. She didn't know exactly where. It could be that they have a friendl rancher south of the bay itself. There are too many things we do not know."

"That we must find out about," Shelter countered. "If we haven't any luck by mid-morning, I suggest we split up into two groups. One can continue to look along the bay, the othe swing inland and ride south."

"What if this corral for the horses is north of the bay?" Raul asked innocently.

Shelter frowned. "All right, then we split into three group and one heads north."

A shout of pleased surprise rose from a trio of men wading barefoot at the water's edge. They held aloft two large irregular dark-gray shells. Long and squarish, thicker by far o the back edge, they reminded Shelter of an axe head.

"*Hachas!*" one of the diggers called out. "Many *hachas*."

"Hatchet clams," Padre Miguel explained. "We are in for treat tonight. They are most tasty. And back a ways, I saw hundreds of rock oysters on those submerged trees that ha drifted in. Wrapped in seaweed and steamed in a pit, they wi make a most noble feast." He looked sternly at those aroun him. "Gluttony is a sin. Being a gourmet is not. If only we had suitable wine to go with them."

Smiling, Ernesto, son of the richest cantinero in Parado reached into a deep pack on one mule and produced two dusty green bottles. "I have the honor of presenting this brave expe dition with twelve bottles of the finest Domecq wines. Si *blanco* and six *tinto*. My father's contribution to our success.

164

"A man after my heart!" the priest exclaimed.

Firewood came at as great a premium as potable water. A wide search produced little, beyond mesquite and manzanita in thin branches that would burn rapidly. Drift wood had to be included to make a suitable fire. Three men quickly dug a deep pit, lined it with the ever-present rocks and kindled a blaze. Darkness had not yet fallen and the supply of clams and oysters had grown to mountainous piles, when one of the complement spied a large barge approaching from the south.

Long sweeps propelled it, manned by four burly men, while a fifth rested his ample buttocks over the stern rail and controlled the big rudder. The owner-captain saw their fire and altered course. Slowly the outsized vessel drew nearer, revealing its unusual construction and proportions for this area.

"*Hola!*" the *barquero* hailed them as he came close in-shore.

"You are in time for a feast," Shelter answered back. "Pull your barge up on the shore and join us."

"*Gracias, Señor.*"

In five minutes the vessel had been beached and the crew broke out large brown bottles of beer, which they distributed to everyone who wanted one. They had hinged metal closing devices and rubber gasketed ceramic stoppers. Shelter gratefully snapped one open and stood back from the fire with the captain and Padre Miguel.

"I am wondering," the captain began. "Are you also passengers for the cove around the point to the south? Your *amigos* have gone on ahead of you. But they instructed me that there would be a *gringo* who would come along after them."

"I am not the one," Shelter allowed after listening to the translation. "But tell me, why is it they go by boat?"

The bargeman shrugged. "It is the only way, *Señor*. The cove is land-locked."

The words heightened Shelter's interest. "Do these men come here often?"

"Oh, *si*. They are *caballeros ricos*, who come to have big

165

parties. They bring their women, spend much money to be taken to and from the cove. So that they may enjoy their stay, my crew and I carry to them supplies of goats, pigs, beans and many cases of tequila and beer. I am on such a run now. I thought you had arrived earlier than expected and wanted you to know I would be able to transport you tomorrow."

"Sorry I am not the man. You are going back there tomorrow?"

"*Si.* I go to the *mercado* at the fishing camp of Paco Nunez for the food and liquor and then start back tomorrow, if everything is loaded. If not, the next day, eh?"

"*Mañana tambien es un otra dia,*" Shelter quoted the expression he had learned typified the lack of haste on the part of people in Mexico.

"*Ay!* You understand well, *Señor.*"

"Although I am not one of their party, I would like to go to this cove, get a look at it. Perhaps my friends and I would hire you to take us there some time when these gentlemen are not using it."

"It would be my pleasure, *Señor.* I can stop for you tomorrow, then?"

"Yes. Or the next day. Whenever."

"I am delighted to do that."

"Ah, Shelter, perhaps I have a suggestion you might want to hear," Padre Miguel said in English. "It might be safer, and more believable, if Raul and I went along as part of the *barquero's* crew. Our friend," he carefully avoided mention of El Guillo's name, "is a suspicious man. He has suffered a defeat recently and will be doubly cautious. Sight of a *Norteño* who is not Plaskoe might arouse him and lessen our chance for success."

"You're right, Padre," Shelter agreed reluctantly. He wanted badly to see the playground of this vicious killer. He also hoped to see some sign that Maria Elena was alive and well.

"Then that is settled?"

"Yes. You two go with the barge tomorrow."

18.

True to the prediction, another day passed before the barge returned. Due to the vast distances to cover, limitations on supply of certain items and the oppressive heat of the Baja desert that made travel in the afternoon hazardous at best, nothing moved fast. One could accept it philosophically, 'Tomorrow is also another day,' or rail against the 'lazy, indolent peons,' as did many *gringos*. Shelter Morgan gained even more respect in the eyes of his companions when he shrugged it off. When the departure at last came, he saddled up his big black and rode off alone to sit on a large boulder and contemplate the bay.

His thoughts turned to Maria Elena. He readily acknowledged that she had a beauty unlike any he had seen before. Something wild and primitive had melded with the aristocratic lines of Castilian Spain. She had a magnificent body. She used it well, with the explosive force of dynamite, in bed. Here was the type of woman he could gladly settle down with. To him it didn't matter that she had known other men.

She was not a cloistered Southern belle of the pre-War times. Virtue meant little, except to the rich, in a country so poor that sex was the only entertainment for many thousands. He had no doubt that he could keep her faithful to him. But where would they live? And when? He had years of hunting down men whose faces remained burned on his brain. He sought more than twenty more.

The shots had hardly echoed away from the ambush site where his men had died in a vain attempt to defend the gold, when Shelter Morgan swore to himself to remember the ones involved in the treachery and exact payment from them in kind for what they did. Many names remained on that mental list. Could he interrupt his search for even a prolonged stay with Maria Elena? Would he be able to face himself if he threw over his plank of revenge in order to spend the rest of his life with her? A pang of sorrow accompanied his answer.

No. He could do neither.

Every day that went by put time and distance between him and the men who must suffer for their deeds. He knew he was neither judge nor jury. That his acts could be, and sometimes had been, considered criminal. He accepted that judgement. It would not deter him. Some day, somewhere, one of the men he stalked might well find him first. A bullet or a knife in the back remained a definite possibility. When it came, if it came, he wanted no one left behind with a burden because of his loss. He sighed heavily and looked out across the sparkling waters.

In late afternoon, a grating clatter brought him out of his reverie. Far in the distance he saw the familiar outline of a high-sided, tall wooden wheeled carreta approaching slowly. Some instinct, nearly feral, caused the hairs to rise on his neck. Shelter went to his horse and led him out of sight. Then he waited among the rocks.

Slowly the cart drew nearer. Some tall, oblong object had been covered by canvas that, in turn, was lashed down tightly. As the primitive conveyance came closer, Shelter had no doubt as to what it might be. He strained his eyes to see the man on the driver's seat. Distance, haze off the water and heat ripples defied his attempts. Finally he recognized the features of an American, rather than some local inhabitant. Immediately he knew who it was.

When the cart came to a stop beside the cluster of boulders, Morgan stepped out into sight, hand on the butt of his Colt. Hot sun, dry, chapping wind and a five day growth of beard had radically altered Shelter's appearance. The man on the wagon looked at him in surprise, though without recognition.

"Un, hello. I didn't expect to see a fellow American around here," Tom Plaskoe greeted the man standing in front of his carreta.

"I've been waiting for you. Sergeant Thomas Plaskoe, you are guilty of robbery from the Confederate States of America and of murder and treason."

"Oh, my God. Morgan. Captain Shelter Morgan. I . . . I thought Mike and Dave took care of you back at the mine."

"They were easy," Shelter said with scorn. "So was that helpless kid you set up in the tunnel."

"Why have you come after me? I'm not the one who planned it. I'm not responsible. The law doesn't want me for what was done."

"I do." Fear washed over Plaskoe's face at Morgan's words. "I've been tracking down those who betrayed the Cause, killed my men and tried to murder me. Colonel Fainer, Major Twyner and his kid brother, Rory Simmons, Nate Lewis . . . I could name more than a dozen others. I've killed each and every one. Now it's your turn."

"General Custis killed himself," Plaskoe challenged, stalling for time.

"That's right. Because he heard I was coming after him. You were all cowards. Backshooters and betrayers. So long as I live, I will make your filthy kind pay."

"What you're doing is against the law." Plaskoe rose and stepped into the back of the carreta. His only hope, he knew, was to reach the Gatling gun. "Listen to me, Cap'n Morgan. I'm a rich man now. I can share it with you. I have a good racket going with some Mexican bandits. In fact, they are supposed to meet me here today. You could find yourself in a lot of trouble if you don't side with me." As he talked, his hands made busy undoing the tie-downs for the cover. He freed the last front one and stepped further back.

"Do you mean El Guillo?" Mention of the name made Plaskoe turn paler white. "He's at the cove. A barge is to come for you. Two of my men are on that barge now. There's no

169

escape for you, Plaskoe."

"Oh, yes there is!" the desperate man yelled as he stepped behind his fearsome weapon and yanked the canvas free. His hand went to the crank.

"Don't be a fool, Plaskoe. That thing might shoot fast, once you get it moving, but I'm a gambling man. I'm willing to bet that I can clear leather and put a slug right between your eyes before the first round falls from the hopper into the breach of the Gatling."

A nervous tic pulled at the corner of Plaskoe's left eye and his mouth. His hand felt wet with sweat and beads of oily fear stood out on his forehead. "For the last time, I'm askin' you. Throw in with me and we'll both be rich. Who gives a damn what happened a few days before the War ended?"

"I do," the cold, grim words lashed at Tom Plaskoe.

For a moment, images of his past four years floated behind Tom Plaskoe's eyes. He stroked the hot flesh of many women, tasted the savory foods of the best establishments in San Diego, fine whiskey, blooded horses. A bank account overflowing with wealth. With a whimper of frightened resignation, he jerked at the crank.

Whiteness exploded in his brain.

From somewhere far off he heard the strident report of the big Colt that had leaped into Shelter Morgan's hand. Thrown backward by the impact, Tom Plaskoe flipped over the tailgate of the carreta and landed in the rocky sand. His eyeballs bulged from their sockets and blood ran from his nose, mouth and both ears. Two hundred fifty-five grains of lead had mushroomed from .45 to seventy caliber and jellied his brain. From somewhere came the scent of violets, sweet and cloying on the air. Darkness seeped in from the sides and a vast numbness padded him from pain.

In a twinkling his last impressions faded. His legs did a death dance against the white grains and, with a mighty convulsion, his body heaved heavenward and gave up his blighted soul.

170

When the excited men from Parador and El Crucero rode up, yelling questions and demanding to know what happened, Shelter Morgan had reholstered his six-gun and answered them quietly, with only a touch of irony in his voice.

"Now *we* have a Gatling gun."

Late the next afternoon, the barge returned. Morgan paid the man and his crew to remain. Already a plan worked in his head. Raul Sanchez bubbled with excitement.

"You have got to see it. It is a magnificent little cove, surrounded by great, high cliffs. Clean beaches, sparkling in the sun, calm water, so clear you can see to the bottom. Many *langostas, abulon,* so much to eat for the taking. The bandits have built palapas for shade and live under them. They are drinking and feasting, dancing and making love with their women. There is a flock of children along. They play in the water, swim and dive for the lobsters and abalone, muscles and oysters. It is a paradise."

"Inhabited by the devil," Shelter growled. "It sounds like you would prefer to rejoin your old *compañero,* eh?"

Raul assumed a wounded expression. "Me? Oh, no, Sheltor. Absolutely not. All the same, it is a beautiful place."

"And completely land-locked?"

"Of a certainty."

"Did . . . did you see Maria Elena?"

"Yes. Once, from a distance. We stayed on the *barca.* She was at the water's edge with a handsome looking little boy of about seven years. Like the others, he was naked as the day he was born. She was teaching him how to swim."

"Whose . . . do you know whose boy he was?"

"No, but Padre Miguel figured he must be important. Two guards stood close by, even more concerned about the child than if she might try to swim to our boat and escape."

"El Guillo's son," Shelter said for no reason he could fathom. It fit, though. Who else would be guarded in so safe a camp? He called his small force together. "Listen. I have a

171

plan. It won't be easy, but we can manage it."

"Everyone gathered around and sat in studied attention, their cool beer and freshly cooked lobsters from the bay forgotten. Shelter made a rough sketch, based on Raul's description of the cove and the sheer cliffs that surrounded it.

"The bandits are here. Camped under palapas. No walls, no parapets to fight from. I want a force of fifteen, under Raul Sanchez's command, to start out immediately for here." His stick pointed at a place behind the western cliff face. "The hard part will be yours, Raul. Can you handle it?"

"El Tiburon can do anything you ask, *amigo*."

"You haven't heard what it is. The remainder will come with me on the barge. El Guillo is expecting Tom Plaskoe and his Gatling gun. The silhouette of the carreta aboard this barge will not be suspicious to any lookouts he has stationed."

"There are only two, one at each point at the mouth of the cove," Padre Miguel provided.

"So much the better. We will sail after dark. That gives you until tomorrow night, Raul, to be in place. You and your men will scale the promontory. Place them well so that they can fire down into the camp on signal. Then you do the most dangerous part."

"What is that?"

"I want you to climb down that cliff, locate Maria Elena and get her to safety on one of the points. Kill the lookouts if you can and build a signal fire to let us know it is ready for us to come in. When I open fire with the Gatling gun, that will be the time for the men on the ridge to open up."

"You mean I am to climb down that cliff? *Ay, amigo!* You did not see that sheer face, *I* did. It is . . . how do you say? Straight down. It is suicide to try it."

"Use some ropes, figure out something."

"But we do not have ropes so long."

"They should have some on the barge. We'll borrow them for you."

172

"*Ay de mi*, to die so young."

"You will do it, though?"

Raul still looked dubious. "For you, my *amigo* . . . I will do anything."

"Good. Gather what you need and ride out with your picked men in fifteen minutes. Tomorrow night we visit El Guillo."

19.

"Are you really going to be my new *Momi*, Maria?"

The question came from a tousel-headed, very sleepy, Pepito Santacruz. The big-eyed child lay on a straw-stuffed mattress ticking pallet under the largest palapa on the shelf behind the cove. Pepito Santacruz's bright, liquid eyes fastened on Maria Elena's face and he fought to keep from falling asleep.

"That's what your father wants," the young captive evaded.

"It's what *I* want, too. You are so beautiful. Just like my real *Momi*."

Flustered, Maria Elena blushed slightly. "How do you know that? I thought you were only a baby when your mother went to the angels."

"*Si*, but *Papi* talked to me a lot about her when I was little and she comes to me in my dreams and tells me about heaven and how happy she is there."

Sympathy and love crimped at Maria's heart. She had never before encountered a small boy with such a poetic soul. How could he be the son of such a *ladron* as El Guillo? She bent and kissed Pepito on the cheek.

"That's beautiful, Pepito. I hope your mother comes to you always." She found herself having to brush at a tear. "Now you go to sleep. Tomorrow is a big day. There's the *barbacoa* and the foot races."

"Don't forget the swimming. You teach me so much better than Juan Rubio used to do. Oh, I love you so, Maria Elena."

Stop it! she thought furiously. Any more and she would bawl like a baby. She gathered her tattered emotions. "Good night,

174

my sweet Pepito."

"'Night, my new *Momi*."

Maria Elena rose and walked out under the stars. How enormous the sky seemed. Even the few night lights of La Rumarosa dimmed them compared to here. Gentle waves lapped on the distant beach and she walked that way. Bare-foot, like all the women and children who came to this cove, she felt the coolness of the sand between her toes when she left the shelf and strolled out toward the low tide line.

"You should not be here alone." It was El Guillo.

"Oh! Ah, you startled me. I was filled with thoughts."

"About what?"

"I . . . I just put Pepito to bed. He's a beautiful child, Rudolfo."

"He takes after his mother. Me . . . I am not so beautiful, no? More like . . . ugly."

"I don't mean his physical appearance, though he is a hand-some boy at that. It's his mind, his soul. Have you ever taken time to listen to him talk about things. Heard him explain his version of how he's come to deal with his mother being dead?"

"Uh . . . as a matter of fact, ah, I have. It makes me . . . it weakens me."

"In other words it makes you want to cry?"

El Guillo drew in a deep breath, then gusted it out in a sigh that carried his answer. "Yes. I want to get him a guitar. One with twelve strings. He has the heart of a Spanish poet."

Maria Elena gasped. "Why . . . that was exactly what I thought when he told me about his mother visiting him in his dreams."

"You see, we are so alike. And Pepito worships, you."

"I know. That's what makes it so hard."

"I'll not always be a bandit. I want so much to . . . to . . ."

Maria Elena raised on tiptoe and kissed the rugged bandido on his right cheek, her hand gently caressing the other. "Let it wait. Love is something that has to grow."

Something had broken the tender mood. El Guillo the out-

175

law chieftan had returned to replace Rudolfo Santacruz the romantic. "How would you know, *puta*? Get back up the strand or I will have to send guards," he growled.

"Rudolfo . . . I . . ."

But he had gone.

Shelter Morgan spent the next day loading the carreta onto Orofino Gilbran's barge. He had selected two young men from El Crucero to train as his crew and, after the sturdy vehicle had been chocked into place, he began their instructions.

"Benito, you will keep the long stick with the swab handy at all times. Every fifteen rounds or so, I will stop firing. You dip the swab in water and run it down all of the barrels. While I am firing, you will be opening ammunition cases for me. Hector, you are the trainer. You sit here and use that crank to move the gun carriage onto targets. Since what we'll be shooting at will mostly be people, you will probably not have much to do. I'll be in free-fire, so the gun will swing where I want it to point. In that case, you will stand by with six rounds of cornmeal loads to scour the barrels every thirty rounds and, when I stop firing for a cleaning, you will dump ammunition in the hopper.

"It goes in the hopper up to here," Morgan went on. "Make sure the cartridges fall in straight, with the noses pointed forward. Load fifteen rounds at a time. No more. That way the gun is clear for cleaning."

Padre Miguel completed his translation and looked at Shelter.

"Questions?"

"Will they be shooting at us?" Hector inquired.

"At first, yes. But remember, we have greater firepower and range. When we open up, we will be out of range of anything they have. With the snipers on the ridge, by the time we get in where their weapons can be effective, there shouldn't be enough of them left to worry about."

"Do we go fight on foot?" Benito wanted to know.

"Eventually. Once the barge grounds at the low tide line we go over the side and attack them from the beach."

Two even, white grins answered this remark. "That is a good thing, I think," Benito said for both of them.

"Yes. When we are too far away to do anything but work that big gun for you while they shoot at us, it is not so much fun as when we get in close enough to use our *cuchillos*."

The remarks dispelled a slight worry Shelter had developed over the wisdom of his choice. He lifted a box of ammunition and examined it. Then he displayed it to the two Mexicans.

"This is how you open a box of cartridges. When you hand it up, make sure that this side always goes first. Then no one can make a mistake, even in the dark. You will feel the ridges in the carton where it was crimped against the wooden case." He passed it around.

"By tonight, you two will be ready to kill a lot of bandidos."

In the darkness caused by a late-rising moon, El Tiburon lay at the lip of the cliff. He peered over, awed by the number of blazing fires and the merriment below. Men and women danced and kissed, or strolled off into the dark to answer more basic urges. Half a beef rotated on a spit, splatters of fat popping to hiss into smoke on the glowing coals below. Another cookfire held three whole goats. Three women sat on rocks around a third, with a thick iron sheet over the fire. They dabbed into a large crockery bowl of dough, rolled small balls from the light tan substance and patted out round, flat tortillas on their bare, exposed thighs. Raul licked his lips. He could almost taste them. The tortillas and those sweet thighs as well. The only drawback was in where he lay. It looked a lot further down than it had from the barge.

He eased back from the treacherous descent and signaled to the other men. It had been an easy ascent. The slope didn't steepen until three-quarters of the way up. It had necessitated leaving their horses behind, under care of a single man. Two men struggled forward with the thick coil of rope.

"We are ready, *Don* Raul," a young *vaquero* whispered.

I'm not, Raul thought to himself. "Good. Come. I will show you where to secure this end."

A lightning-blasted Boojum tree trunk clung to the slope ten feet back from the rim. Raul supervised the secure tying of the rope to its girth and tested it with a stout pull. He turned the coil over then and fashioned a manner of seat in it. As he worked he explained to the men.

"I will sit in this sling and hold onto the rope. When I signal, you will let it over the side slowly. Then pay out the remaining rope. When I get to the bottom, I will give a strong yank. There is, I hope, enough to make it."

"You are going now?"

"No. We will wait until it grows quieter. Some *cabron* might look up at that cliff and in all that firelight I'd be seen easy as that." He snapped his fingers. "Five or six hours, *muchachos*. We can sleep until ten. I want guards put to watch and to wake us when the time comes. You two, Jaime and Duran. One to keep an eye on the *bandidos* below, the other to watch our back trail. Wake us in five hours."

When Jaime gently shook his shoulder, Raul nearly leaped off the side of the hill. He quickly calmed himself and tried to summon his courage. Duran met them at the edge of the cliff.

"The fires have burned low. Most of the men and a lot of the women are *borracho*. The ones still up stagger around in the sand like blind men." Duran snickered. "If they only knew."

"You can thank *el Dio bueno*, that they do not, *amigo*, or they would be long gone and we would be in for trouble," Raul told him.

"*Mas o meno*. Will the barge be in place?"

"Of course. You can trust Shel-tor to do everything right. I . . . I trained him myself."

"*Mierda*. He is a soldier, you can tell it in the way he walks."

"And the way Padre Miguel introduced him in your village of Parador, no?"

"You have taken the *Jotas*," Duran relented. "But I will throw *Aces*."

"We are not playing dice here, *amigo*. This is serious business."

"*Verdad*," Jaime agreed, getting into the kidding. "You could be shot off that rope like a swinging target in a booth at the *faria*, no?"

"Why do you remind me of such a horrible fate, Jaime?"

"Because I like you, Raul."

The former bandit, El Tiburon, sighed heavily. "It is time to go."

He got into the harness and scuttled backward to the edge. "Wake the rest of the men, so they can be ready. Where are the two who will lower me?"

"Right here, *Jefe*."

"Well, then . . . I suppose we had better start."

The first fifty feet went easily. Raul hung out in space, some fifteen feet from the cliff face and eased smoothly downward. A light, on-shore breeze sprang up and ruffled his hair. He had left his sombrero behind for fear it might blow off and reveal his presence. He kept swallowing rapidly and his hands, where he gripped the rope above his head, trembled slightly. He descended another ten feet and the cliff seemed to leap outward at him.

"*Dios!*" he gasped in a soft whisper.

The optical illusion had been so real he nearly lost his grip. Raul took another deep breath and reached out with one hand to fend off the rocks that slid slowly past his face. Why had he ever agreed to this? The question kept recurring the further he went down. Enough rope had payed out now that the hand over hand motion of the men lowering him transmitted to him as solid jerks, which he visualized as easily unseating him and sending his body tumbling helplessly to his death a hundred feet below. The rope lurched again.

"If I ever get out of this," he promised himself in a barely audible murmur, "I'll never volunteer for anything again in

179

my life."

"Shove hard, then everyone get on board when the keel
breaks free," Orofino Gilbran instructed the six unusual
customers he had agreed to help.

With a mighty heave, the barge came loose from the sand
and bobbed in the calm waters of Bahia de Los Angeles.
Quickly the small combat team scrambled over the low sides of
the barge and found places to sit.

"It is a dark night," Shelter Morgan observed to the boat
man.

"Yes. I would like it better if the moon had risen before we
left."

"Why is that? Wouldn't that let El Guillo's men see us
better?"

"It would also let me see dangerous rocks better," Orofino
observed. "That way we might stay afloat with the bottom not
ripped out of this ancient barge."

"Somehow," Shelter mused, "that fails to comfort me."

The sweeps moved rhythmically, manned by two rowers
each this time, cutting them through the still water of the bay
with far greater speed than ordinary. When an on-shore breeze
riffled up out of the east, the water took on a bit of a chop.
Shelter felt his stomach lurch and his head reeled a moment.
Around him he heard groans from the land-based men he had
brought here.

"Hold on to your suppers, men," he urged through Padre
Miguel's interpretation. "You'll need them for energy when
we get there."

"D-don't even think about food," Andres complained from
where he manned an oar. "To talk about it is worse. It only
invites it to come u . . . urup!" With a helpless gulping sound,
Andres rose and leaned far over the side of the barge.

"Feeding the fish will not get the barge there quickly,"
Orofino advised from his position at the helm. A hint of

180

suppressed laughter sounded in his words. "Why is it that men who live on the land can never stand the least bit of roughness at sea? I have seen butchers who wade in guts and blood all day turn green and spew up everything they have eaten for a week."

Two more of the fighting men leaned over the rail to disgorge their last meal. For a long moment, Shelter Morgan thought he would join them. The queasy feeling in his stomach persisted and he fought it by swallowing.

"Don't do that, *amigo*," Orofino advised. "Not without something to take down. Here, try an old tortilla. Chew it fine, then swallow."

Shell found it worked marvelously. Although the swells deepened and the blunt nose of the barge rose, swayed left and right before dropping and flung bits of spray over the deck, he discovered that the added weight of the tortilla on his disturbed stomach calmed it. When he regained most of his composure, he went about distributing tortillas to Padre Miguel and the other four men.

"At this speed," Orofino told him when he returned to the stern rail, "we will be there two hours before dawn."

Something went terribly wrong above when Raul reached a point some fifteen feet from the base of the cliff. His descent went from utter slowness to blurring speed. Instinctively he reached out with his hand and both feet. When they made contact with the bulging face of rock, he bent both knees and flexed strongly outward.

His wise maneuver saved him a good deal of pain. He hit sand instead of rocks, albeit with force enough to jar the wind out of his lungs. He sprawled, gasping, on the firmly packed strand and waited, fearful that at any moment an alert sentry would rush over to blast out his brains.

Instead, he heard nothing except the distant, drunkenly slurred voice of an amorous bandit singing a love ballad. Footsteps churned the sand fifty feet away and he hugged the dark shadows formed by rocks that surrounded the small clearing where he had landed. Rocks! Their presence prevented his discovery, yet thought of them and his headlong plummet down the last few feet sent shivers up his spine. So far luck had stayed with him. From his left he heard the whispery splatter of a man relieving himself. It went on a long time, then the footsteps moved away from the rocks.

"*Buenas suerte,*" he muttered to himself, wishing his good luck to continue. Raul rose to a crouch and darted forward across the sand.

Near the first palapa, he discovered a drunken bandido, sleeping off his over-indulgence. An inch from the *borracho's* outflung arm lay a half-full bottle of tequila. Thankfully Raul retrieved it and the man's sombrero. Then he stood upright and staggered out among the scattered forms of sleeping or passed out bandits and their women.

In a random manner, he continued to stumble about like the few upright outlaws while he checked each palapa to locate Maria Elena.

"*Hola,*" a voice summoned him. "It looks like we are the only ones who can hold their tequila, eh?"

"Too true, *amigo,*" Raul slurred back. "I'm going to go take a piss."

"Don't take too long. Consuelo is giving *chupona* to anyone who can stand still without weaving. And you know how good her lips are."

"*Ay de mi!* I shall hurry then," Raul promised as he weaved his way out into the darkness in character with his words. Fine. All he needed right then was a blow job, Raul thought as he worked his way around to continue his search from another angle.

His quest took longer than he had expected. At last he found Maria Elena fast asleep in one corner of the largest palapa. Near her lay a remarkably handsome little boy, his childish lips upcurved in a sweet smile of innocence. Maria Elena did not seem nearly so pure in heart. Her face retained the flushed fullness of recent passion and she slept naked on a mat, a thin blanket spread over her lower body and legs. Slowly, taking care to be utterly silent, Raul knelt at her side.

He placed his hand lightly over her mouth and with the other, shook her shoulder. She stirred and began to mutter.

"Not again, Rudolfo. Don't you ever get enough?"

"Quiet," Raul barely breathed out. He clapped his hand tightly on her lips. "It is I, Raul Sanchez. I have come to take you to a safe place."

Still half-asleep, Maria Elena struggled a moment until her eyes focused on Raul's narrow face and deep, sincere eyes. Shelter Morgan had sent him to rescue her! she thought in sudden excitement. She nodded and the hand came from her mouth. With slow movements, she slid from under the blanket and reached for her clothes.

Raul gasped in erotic amazement. What a beautiful *nalga*, such lovely titties. *Ay*, Shel-tor has all the luck where it counts. Such a beautiful one. She slid into a thin cotton dress, disdained shoes, and cast a worried look in the direction of El Guillo. He slept soundly, albeit with a huge erection lifting the woolen cover over his hips. Raul, still entranced by her lithe pulchritude, motioned her to follow.

A dozen yards into the dark, Maria Elena clutched at Raul's arm and signaled him to halt. "What is going on?" she whispered.

Quickly Raul explained Shelter Morgan's plan. He concluded with an urgent appeal. "So we must get you away to safety quickly. Then I will kill the sentries at the mouth of the cove and signal Shel-tor to come in."

"We can't."

"What do you mean?"

"Not without taking Pepito along. He is a sweet little boy and I couldn't bear to see him killed like that."

"He is El Guillo's brat," Raul said sternly.

"Pepito is not like that. Anyone who sees him, loves him. He is bright and talks almost like a poet writes words."

"*Dios!* A romantic bandit's spawn. Think sensibly, woman."

"I am. Pepito deserves a better chance than living and dying with bandidos. Please, Raul. I can waken him and he will come along if I say so."

"You are assuring our deaths, *chiquita.*"

"No I am not." Maria Elena stood in a defiant posture, fists on hips. "Either he comes or I stay to protect him."

"Shel-tor said to see you were safe. To do that you have to come with me."

"Not without Pepito."

"Damn it, woman . . ." He sighed in resignation. "As you say, then. Go get the boy."

Maria returned to the palapa and knelt beside Pepito Santacruz's pallet. She put a hand over his mouth and shook the youngster. When his eyes opened, she placed a finger over her mouth to signify silence, then bent and whispered in his ear.

"We're going to play a game. It will be a surprise for your father. Get out of bed. Bring your *pantalones*, but don't take time to put them on. We're going to meet a man outside who will help us hide."

Pepito nodded vigorously. He understood the hiding game. It would be a big joke on his father. He slid from the mat, grabbed up his knee-length trousers and padded barefoot and naked after Maria Elena. His sweet smile drove a sudden spike of guilt through her heart.

She was helping to kill a man who had asked her to be his wife. A man she had slept with not at all unwillingly. To the worse of the bargain, she was aiding in a deception of an innocent child. Would Pepito hate her when the killing was over and he learned the truth? For a moment she wanted to stop, turn around and hurry back to warn Rudolfo Santacruz of the danger that lurked all around the festive camp.

Then she pictured the depredations of the bandits in La

Rumarosa, El Crucero and half a dozen other villages. She forced herself to harden her heart, close out of her mind any considerations but doing what Shelter Morgan had asked of her.

Raul joined them in the darkness of a shadowed boulder. He had gathered some wood and a scrap of paper. Without words he pointed them toward the extended arm of land at that side of the cove. They walked in silence.

Near the tip of the small sand sprit, Raul waved them down. He crept forward and, unseen by the child, drew a knife from his belt scabbard. A lone sentry leaned against a large rock, eyes droopy with sleep and alcohol, and gazed out to sea. He yawned and his head nodded. Raul slithered into position and, with a deep insuck of breath, struck.

The knife sunk into the hollow of the guard's throat. He thrashed about and tried to force air past the metalic obstruction that had severed his windpipe and now lashed at the cords of muscle and vital blood vessels. Slowly his struggles weakened and ceased.

Raul removed his knife, wiped it and his bloody hand and forearm on the dead bandit's shirt. He returned for the small bundle of wood he had appropriated. When he squatted beside Maria Elena and Pepito, his eyes scanned the surrounding terrain as best possible in the darkness, relieved only by distant, frosty starlight. He saw a shadowy depression a few yards away.

"There," he whispered. "Take the boy and hide in that bowl. Don't . . ." a long suppressed vein of softness tempered his words, "don't let him see what is going on."

"Oh, my God!" Maria Elena whispered. She fought to hold back tears, not for herself or El Guillo, but for Pepito. Quickly she and the boy moved off across the sand. Raul returned to the point with his firewood.

He quickly split kindling with his knife and placed it on the bit of paper, then added more solid pieces. By his estimation, it was nearly time. The moon would rise in half an hour. That would make it less than two hours before dawn. That's when he would light the fire.

"Maria?" El Guillo muttered. He groped the space next to him, found nothing and sat up. His phallus had become engorged to an aching extent and he needed soothing. He looked around but could not see her.

"Maria!" he called again. No answer. Then he saw not only her sleeping place empty, but that of his son. "Pepito! Where are you, boy?" He rose, naked and uncaring. "Maria come back here."

Others among the bandits began to awaken. One of them spotted the unusual fire burning on the far tip of one breakwater that formed the cove.

"Who is out there with a fire, *Jefe?*" the liquor-sodden bandit asked.

"I . . . don't know. Has anyone seen Maria Elena or Pepito?" Only blank looks and shakes of the head answered him. "Well then, get to looking, you stupid *pendejos!* Find them!"

Bandits ran in every direction, seeking to do their leader's bidding.

"And put out that damned fire."

Others hurried to obey, only to rush into a hailstorm of lead as Shelter Morgan opened up with the Gatling gun.

20.

Blood, bone and intestines filled the night air with a crimson spray.

Shots immediately rained down from the cliff. Women screamed and ran in panic, their children forgotten, left to cower and shriek or race blindly through the turmoil that brought the reality of Hell into their young lives. Several died accidentally by running into the paths of bullets. Slowly, the intoxicated bandits began to recover their wits and return fire.

On the barge, Shelter Morgan cranked the Gatling gun in smooth, even turns, listening to the metalic clinks and solid detonations of the large cartridges. Every fifteen he paused for a cleaning, then ran through more sheets of leaden death. Gradually the barge moved closer.

Six bandidos knelt on the wet sand at the water's edge. They took careful aim and fired at the approaching apparition of a floating cart with death spitting from atop it.

Bullets cracked past Shell's head and he paused to let Hector insert the cornmeal loads. They made a dull sound, compared to live ammunition, the rough grains sweeping deposits of black powder from the hot steel tubes. He nodded for more ammunition and it rattled into the hopper.

"It's the *gringo!*" a man ashore shouted. "He has gone mad."

"Kill him!" El Guillo screamed, visualizing a frothing-mouthed Tom Plaskoe. "Get that *hijo de puta!*"

Shell turned the crank again and a stream of bullets plowed up sand, then kissed flesh. The six bandits exploded at the impact, their bodies ripped and torn by the massive projectiles. Only one survived, for a moment, his leg blown off, blood spurting from severed arteries to soak into the sand. His wails could be heard over the crackle of gunfire from the camp and the cliff above it.

Sand grated against the keel and the barge halted with a lurch. Swiftly, Shelter cranked out a double hopper without pausing to have the gun cleaned. A single bright, brass casing remained to fall into a waiting chamber when the Gatling gun hung up.

By now fires had spread in the camp, blazing fronds making torches of the palapas. Morgan took stock and waved to his small force.

"Rifles at the ready. Let's go," he commanded.

Shelter, Padre Miguel and the rest leaped into the shallow water and charged ashore. A naked bandit rushed at them, armed only with a machete. Padre Miguel lifted his .577 Martini-Henry falling block rifle and blasted the man in his breast bone. The five hundred grain bullet, propelled by eighty grains of black powder, disintegrated the bandido's spine before it blew a big hole out the back in a shower of gore. The priest's lips moved and Shelter wondered at his words.

"Forgive them, Father, they know not what they do."

The sudden swirl of battle divided the men. In the distance, Shelter saw the big mustache and ample girth of El Guillo and sought to work his way there. Bullets whipped past him and dug gouges in the sand at his feet. Men screamed and died all around. Slowly the number of answering rounds diminished. He could only hope that the riflemen on the cliff would know when to stop firing.

A billow of smoke rolled between Shelter and El Guillo. When it cleared the bandit had disappeared. Then Shell caught sight of him running along a narrow sprit of land toward where the signal fire had been burning. Sand clung to his feet while the ex-Confederate labored to close the gap between him and the bandit who had slaughtered so many of the innocent and

188

whipped Maria Elena like a dog.

"Papi!" a shrill child's voice called from a short distance away on the dune.

El Guillo skidded to a halt, whirled and fired instinctively.

In the split second it took, Shelter Morgan ran within fifteen yards of the bandit leader. A familiar voice added speed to his dragging feet.

"Ay, no! Santa Maria, no!" Maria Elena shrieked, her voice breaking with horror and grief. *"Caro Jesus*, you have killed your son, Rudolfo!"

A great cry of anguish ripped from El Guillo's throat. He stumbled, went to his knees, then began to crawl on all fours, his big Dragoon pistols forgotten. Shelter Morgan ran up close to him, intent on putting a .44-40 slug in his left ear. The crazed expression of unassuagable grief that twisted El Guillo's face caused him to pause.

Panting heavily enough to be heard above the tumult of the battle, El Guillo, with Shell walking at his side, continued on hands and knees to the shallow depression in the sand. There, they found Maria Elena.

She sat rocking back and forth, eyes blank, a pitiful keening coming from deep in her throat. In her lap she held a small boy's head. His eyes were open and feverish bright. His face pale as a shroud. A big bullet hole in his chest seeped blood and bubbles from his punctured right lung. Maria Elena seemed not to know the two men had reached her.

"P-papi shot me . . ."* Pepito Santacruz gasped out in a gurgling voice. *"He . . . didn't . . . mea . . ."* His eyes rolled up in their sockets, the wonderously large, shining black pupils dimmed forever and he sighed softly as life left his thin body.

El Guillo fled into the deep recesses of his mind. All that was left was Rudolfo Santacruz, deeply ravaged by the horror of his accidental deed. His haggard face turned tombstone gray and he trembled all over.

"Noooo!" he howled. *"Dios salvami!* I am a monster!" His eyes, jerking wildly from point to point, settled on Shelter

189

Morgan. "Kill me. For the love of Christ, kill me. I can not bear this horrible crime. Kill me, *Señor*, for surely I am damned forever."

Shelter raised the muzzle of his Winchester toward El Guillo's forehead, then paused. "No. I don't think I will. I'm going to let you live with this the rest of your miserable life."

Lightning quick, El Guillo's hands lashed out and seized the barrel of the Winchester. Like a starving child with his mother's tit, he trust the muzzle into his mouth. His violent jerk caused Shelter's finger to tighten on the trigger.

Bone and flesh muffled the report, but could not contain the gush of hot gasses. El Guillo's head burst like a dynamited watermelon. Sprays of fluid, blood and brain matter flew in all directions.

Alerted by the close-by gunshots, Raul Sanchez ran up and surveyed the scene. He stood beside Shelter, staring down at the dead boy and weeping unashamedly. Momentarily sickened, Shelter Morgan turned away, only to be confronted by the haunted face of Maria Elena.

It would take a long time, he knew, to erase this horrible scene from her mind. The healing process would be slow and would take a lot of love. He no longer questioned if he would take time off from his search to spend with the lovely girl. He asked not how long. When it was done, when Maria Elena smiled again and recalled the little boy only in pleasant memories he would know his task had ended.

Where, he wondered, would his endless search take him then?